Watermelon Guy

Tanner Cowgill

Fulton Books, Inc.
Meadville, PA

Published by Fulton Books 2021

ISBN 978-1-63860-797-7 (paperback)
ISBN 978-1-63860-798-4 (digital)

Printed in the United States of America

ACKNOWLEDGEMENTS

There are so many people to thank, and only one
page to thank them on. But, here goes nothing…

Thank you to Jordyn Marie Adkins for allowing me to
use the name she was given at birth—it is a pretty one.

Thank you to the girl who wore the watermelon
dress, inspiring me just enough to write a gosh
darn book about it (you know who you are).

Thank you to everyone who read my novel prior of its
release-the constructive criticism was extremely valuable.

Thank you to my family. You continue loving me,
even though I am hard to love once and awhile.

Lastly, thank you to watermelons everywhere. It's difficult to
understand why things happen to us, but there's always a reason.

I appreciate you all and thank you to everyone who is reading.

High school is tough. People tend to dread it because they haven't found the certain niche they're destined to be in, and others dread it because they simply don't *enjoy* school. My high school follows the certain stigma of other schools: the theatre kids, jocks, goths, and burnouts roam the halls, attempting to "survive" what high school has to offer.

Others dread it because not only have they not found their niche, but they don't belong in one. They're not musically inclined, nor talented in athletics. They don't smoke behind the baseball diamond when they're skipping class or believe in the arts. Some don't do that stuff. Actually, a lot of us don't.

And even though I don't fit into the high school scene, doesn't mean I don't have a niche I belong in. Fortunately for me, there are a lot of us who fucking suck at all the things that you're supposed to care about in high school, so I don't belong in any niche, which allows me to create my own, "The Ones Who Suck." I'm the leader of this specific niche and the others follow me and do whatever I ask them to—like bring me No. 2 pencils or bring me fresh, juicy watermelon at the "End of the Quarter" picnic our school puts on. High school would be a disaster if it wasn't for my friends, who are also members of the fake club we've created. High school would be horrible for all of us if we didn't have each another. The people who are niche-less, forming their own niche. Sort of poetic for some; mostly pathetic for everyone else, but I don't care.

We attempt to survive high school together, sleepwalking from class to class, receiving a mediocre education and learning about subjects we'll never use again by teachers who are rethinking the career paths they've chosen to take—a salary in which they cannot live comfortably, lucky enough to have three meals a day and rent a one-bedroom apartment for their partner and themselves. That's if someone actually chooses to date/marry a teacher with the money they're bringing per year. A nice vacation is going to the Ohio State fair and watching Jeff Dunham perform a comedy skit with him and his best pal, Achmed, while eating corndogs and funnel cakes. This is considered fun for many or punishment for others, depending how you look at it.

I don't have a lot of friends. To be honest, I don't want a lot of friends. People typically say this because people hate them anyway so that's the reason why they don't have any friends. But for me, I genuinely hate 80 percent of the human population. So a lot of friends seems overrated.

I know a lot of people at my school—their tendencies, love life, class schedules, friends and ex-friends—pretty much everything a high schooler can know about their classmates, I know. Rather than walking the hallways with my eyes staring at my phone or listening to music through my headphones, I watch and listen, in a non-creepy sort of way. Watching Bailey go to science in-between third and fourth period. Noticing Emily and Brandon making out at Brandon's locker in-between seventh and eighth because they both have study hall the following period.

Not many people know me, which I don't mind. I like it that way. I don't like others who must show their life to others. They feel like it's a necessity to prove to the outside world they're enjoying their lives and have lots of friends, and they need to flaunt it on social media. We understand and don't care. It's so irritating constantly looking at people who think unimportant things are important.

Life being a teenager is simple. Find friends. Enjoy friends. Do things with friends that make you happy. Not many teenagers discover how easy it really is. People my age tend to lash out because "no one understands them," which I find very funny because everyone gets teenagers—especially adults because they were once a teenager at a point of their lives. It's no secret. We attempt to become things we aren't—posers or something—and it doesn't make any sense. I feel very bad for people who do this. For people who have friends but lose them when they do something irrational or stupid. For people who don't appreciate what they have. People always want more, and I don't like that about the human species.

Summer starts today, and I am very excited. I've heard the summer before senior year is the best. Someone must've taken a vote or created a census because I've heard a lot of people in the hallway saying this. The summer before senior year means the last time to do high school shit before you have to start "growing up."

Senior year means I must begin looking for colleges and searching for a "purpose." That's what my mom has been telling me since I've walked through the front door today after getting back from school. Even though she's been dropping hints since sophomore year, today's tone seemed more real, almost like it's right around the corner. But I'm still thinking about what that exactly means. I can't have a purpose in life. I stick to the basics. I don't do anything outside my comfort zone because it makes me very uncomfortable—which makes me sound like a dumbass—but it's very true. Sticking to the basics means I won't get hurt. And not getting hurt is equivalent to a happy and content life.

But for starters, I'm hoping this summer lasts a lifetime, because I need it to. I'm not ready to grow up and be a college kid. College kids drink and have sex and live away from their mothers. Plus, college kids don't remember their high school friends. That's a type of place that scares me. And a kid like me doesn't belong in a place like that.

June 3, 2017

"You going to that party tonight?" Jake asks me, his red rosy cheeks becoming more obvious with every word. I speculate it's because of his excitement that school has just gotten out for the summer. Or perhaps he's just a fat piece of shit who needs to lose fifteen to twenty pounds. We're sitting in my living room, a bowl of Cool Ranch Doritos sitting in front of Jake's eyes. He tends to eat a lot and not work out, embracing the whole fat-ass persona. His stumpy fingers tend to reach for the bowl more frequently than they're supposed to.

"Are you kidding?" I respond to this idiotic question. "It's Jaret Miller's party." Jaret Miller, who is the captain of the baseball team, is also the *it* child of Worthington, Ohio. All the parents in the city wish their child was like Jaret Miller, which in my opinion is totally ridiculous because they don't know half the dumb shit Jaret Miller does. I've gone to school with him for fourteen years, and my perspective of him is the most accurate. And let me just say, my mother should be thankful that I'm her son and not Jaret Miller. Excluding the fact that Jaret Miller is the whitest name on the planet, besides Keith Cole.

Jaret Miller isn't a normal bully like in the movies who pins kids against lockers and shakes them for their lunch money; he's a modern-day bully. He understands he's better-looking, more athletic, and just overall better than everyone else. He's never been told no by anyone. His parents are millionaires who wanted to give him the "public school experience." He just makes kids feel bad about themselves, not even doing it purposefully half the time. It's just who he is.

"Yes, I'm aware it's Jaret Miller's party," Jake answers, but not before he takes a couple more handfuls of Doritos and shove them

down his hole. "It's the only party that we truly have been invited to."
True, I suppose.

"I tutored Ian last year in English. And Math. And US History.
He's not the brightest." Also true. "But, he promised me an invitation to the first party of the summer, and I can take anyone I want.
Hence why I'm telling you."

In utter amazement, I look at him wide-eyed and mumble out,
"Hence?" It's the smartest thing he has said. This might seem like a
bold statement, but Jake's vocabulary is limited.

"Yes, *hence*," he says. "Ms. Ruiz told me I needed better transitions in my English papers, and *hence* is one she strongly recommended I use. It means *for this reason.*"

"I know what *hence* means Jake. I'm just truly shocked you used
this correctly in a real sentence."

After going back and forth for a little longer, ideas flutter
through my head. Is going to a party worth the possible humiliation and name-calling? Yes, it's a real party. No, I've never been to
a real party, birthdays excluded. No one will know us there. We'll
know everyone. It's nothing different. It's like going to school, except
there will be "liquid gold" and illegal drugs; *fun* for the typical high
schooler. I've seen enough high school films to know what goes on at
parties: sex, illegal drug use, underage drinking, and fights that end
with a liquor bottle getting shattered on someone's thick skull.

"You really want to go?" I ask Jake, pondering over the idea for
a few minutes. The silence didn't bother him too much. Jake was a
little too preoccupied continuing to eat his Doritos, sucking his fingertips every four or five handfuls.

"Of course, I do," he responds. "Besides, if we get lucky, we will
catch some serious ass."

And I laugh after he says this because Jake always finds a way to
turn the littlest of conversations into something sexual, always thinking
with his dick rather than his brain. Which is ironic because Jake is the
one who hasn't gotten some since sophomore year in the candle aisle at
Speedway; that time being the only time he's had sexual relations. The
ones who know, know, and the ones who don't know will never know.
Even the ones who know still doubt the validity of Jake's story. But at

the end of the day, all we have is each other's word. One simply doesn't really *know* anything. All we do is believe what we're told.

"Okay, we'll go," I tell him, after thinking about it for a little longer, allowing more time for Jake to finish the bowl of Doritos that has now moved from in front of him to directly beside him. "But we need to invite the others. If we're going to this party, all of us should experience it."

"Absolutely! Couldn't agree more!" Jake yells, jumping to his feet and rushing out the door. "See you in a couple hours!"

He's gone in an instant. Well, time is relative because his fat-ass doesn't really move extremely fast; it sort of wobbles out the door. Jake is one of many words. Most of the time I get tired of hearing his voice. He loves the spotlight, yet turtles in his shell when he's around anyone but us. He was always the one to suggest kiss the bottle at birthday parties but chickened out when it was his turn. He suggested tee-peeing houses on Halloween rather than going trick-or-treating like all the other middle school kids... And yes, in Worthington, Ohio, trick-or-treat in seventh grade is the norm.

Jake's my best friend, though. We've been best pals for as long as I can remember. He actually understands and enjoys my company. He genuinely likes me, which I can't say for many other people.

*****

It's nice having the house to myself once in a while because it doesn't happen very often. I like spending time in my room. So when the rest of my family is gone, I get to spend time in my room without any disturbances. Like, "Clean the dishes," or "Why don't you do something productive with yourself?" Stuff like that is mostly from my mom.

I've got the smallest bedroom in the house, which doesn't make sense in the slightest because I'm the oldest child. It's a tad bigger than Harry Potter's closet the Dursleys made him sleep in. It also doesn't have the spiders and dust bunnies Harry's closet had. So overall, I don't complain too much. A twin-size bed, a sheet, and comforter is all I need to fulfill my needs in the bedroom.

The doorbell rings, and my clock with a picture of SpongeBob in the middle of it from when I was a kid reads nine. The door opens, and I hear more than one pair of footsteps, meaning Jake must have brought the others.

"Yo, bitch!" Jake yells at the top of his lungs. Followed by, "Get your ass down here!"

Lindsey is not going to like that...she does not find the word *bitch* funny nor amusing. Why is the word *bitch* only referred to girls? Also, why are girls only offended when someone calls them a bitch? Girls can call girls bitches, but when another girl calls them a bitch, they get upset and World War III begins to show signs of appearing? I'm still unclear on how this all works.

I rush downstairs and notice Lindsey, Nick, and Drew accompanying Jake in the kitchen. Jake shoving his face in the fridge while getting an earful from Lindsey, telling him why it is not polite to call someone a bitch.

"You know I hate that word," she says, looking at him with her eyes wide open. "I've told you this. It means a girl dog. And I don't really want you to call anyone a girl dog because that is implying you think of them as a dog, which is not very nice, is it? Plus, I wouldn't think you'd like being called Jelly Roll Jake or Porky Pig, would you?"

Nick and Drew begin snickering, but Jake isn't paying attention. He rarely does, especially to Lindsey. "Yeah, I'm sorry. Truly." False. He isn't sorry. Which turns out to be fine because Lindsey ignores the fake apology and begins speaking, starting another conversation unrelated to the word *bitch*.

"What's up, man?" she asks, walking over and hugging me. "You ready for your first big boy party?" Lindsey is bigger than me—which isn't saying much because I'm 110 pounds with my clothes soaking wet—making her hug suffocating. She also towers over me, so my head is squished in between God's greatest creation—breasts. God, they're lovely. Every pair besides Lindsey's boobs, though.

"Of course," I say, my voice muffled because of the boobs in my face, clearly feeling the opposite. I'm extremely not ready for my first "big boy" party. Jaret Miller, star of the school. His little posse right by his side, hands in their pockets, hats on backward—the ultimate sign of a cool posse. I've never talked to Ian, either, who's a little less intimidating, partially because of the pimples living on his face and partially because of the way he carries himself. Yes, he's a dumbass and can't spell his name, but he looks like a normal student who doesn't get caught up in the high school shit. And that's what it is—high school shit. Opposed to Jaret Miller who looks like a fucking offspring of George Clooney and Mila Kunis.

Lindsey releases me from her grasp and allows me time to catch my breath. "It's okay, dude. It'll be fun. Parties are a time to let loose and not be so uptight. You'll see."

"And you have a lot of prior experience?" Nick asks. Nick, who probably talks the least amongst us, is a tall guy, about six foot four inches. He's strong too. He's the one who doesn't appear like he belongs in our friend group. Based off prior stereotypes created by the ones that came before us, he would be placed in the jock niche. But if someone has a conversation with him for at least five minutes, they'll soon understand... Awkward is an understatement while describing Nick. This is a coping mechanism for his fucked up childhood.

Nick is adopted. When he was really young, his dad liked to beat up his mom. She took it and took it until one day the neighbor walked in while it was happening. He immediately called Children's Services. But the mom was a drug addict who also wasn't fit to take care of a child; she couldn't even take care of herself. So Nick was handed off to his grandparents.

When Nick was eight years old, his grandfather got really sick. The type of sick old people get—dementia and Alzheimer's. Nick's grandmother was committed to taking care of him, though; giving him his medication, spoon-feeding him every hour meant another problem. But she dedicated her life to taking care of him, respectfully upholding her commitment to "till death do us part."

One-night Nick's grandfather was saying some horrible things: How he wanted to die, and he needed his life to end. They had a gun hidden in their closet. Nick's grandmother rushed to the closet, as fast as elderly people can go, trying to get the gun as far away as possible.

But it was too late. Nick's grandfather already had the gun and shot himself directly in front of his wife, who saw the whole thing go down. One can only imagine, and can't even put into words the horrible, traumatic event it was. No one should ever have to endure what she must've seen, especially a woman who loved so deeply the man she spent her entire life with.

Nick's grandmother was placed in a mental institution, suffering from PTSD, and Nick was placed in foster homes until a really nice family decided to adopt him—the current household where he lives now.

Nick had been friends with us for a while until he decided to tell us what happened. He keeps to himself. He's had a horrible, tragic life up until he met us. He cares for us. He loves us. And if we can make him feel happiness and joy just by talking and spending time with him, that is what we need to do.

Lindsey answers Nick's question about her frequent party crasher alter ego by saying, "I've been to dozens of parties. One time, a couple years ago, I went to a party at Jaret Miller's house. After Homecoming I think, sophomore year."

"Didn't you say you had curfew that night?" Drew blurts out. "That's why you didn't come to my house, right?"

"Indeed, Drew, indeed. I decided to ditch you guys to see what life was like being a *cool kid*." Lindsey puts air quotes around *cool kid*, easing my worries. I thought for a second that we had different definitions of what it meant to be a cool kid.

The four of us look at one another, puzzled, Lindsey excluded.

"You shitting me?" I say to her. "Isn't our whole friend group still friends because we never lie to each other. Isn't that our thing?" And it is our thing. This one time, I was forced to tell my friends about my first boner because it was such a "turning point" in a "young man's life." It goes without saying, it was a tad embarrassing. But a boner is still a boner, even if Mrs. Incredible was the one who caused it. And let me add, that woman is a bad bitch.

"Oh, relax," Lindsey starts. "Just one time, you have to be willing to take a risk and create some drama within the friend group. That was my one time and I'm never doing it again. Promise. Besides… I meant the love of my life there. A fucking 10/10."

"And?" we all say in unison, waiting for Lindsey to expand on her comment. Because this is the first time we're hearing about the "love of her life." This would be the second "love of her life," and coincidently, the first was Mrs. Incredible. Again, the woman just has her way with the audience.

"Oh, don't worry about her. We went our different ways. I'm saving myself for one of you three to take my hand in marriage and be the most depressed wife in the history of depressed wives."

It's true. Thinking about a life with Lindsey is oddly unsettling, even though she's one of my closest friends. Plus, I don't think she would be good at giving oral pleasure. A guy just knows these things.

We sit there for a while, talking about shit that doesn't matter. Shit that rarely gets said aloud. Topics include: why romantic comedies are the best genre of movie, hats serve no purpose other than protecting bald spots on grown adult heads, and Columbus Day being the most underrated holiday in human history (And the ones who consider Columbus Day, Indigenous People's Day can go to hell). Don't blame me for my beliefs. Blame my parents for making me like this.

Talking about this shit is beyond pointless, but it's what we do. In my eyes, every friend group talks about nothing and enjoys it. Maybe I'm wrong. It just seems like no friend group sits in a circle and chats about foreign policy or how well the economy is doing. No way in fuck. What they *talk* about is how to get laid and what type of Dorito is the best... Cool Ranch, clearly.

When it comes time for us to leave, we pile in the Green Saturn that sits four but fits five and drive away. Jake brings along some tiny slices of pepperoni for the ride over, which smell horribly. He says, "Who doesn't like pepperoni?" and no one replies because nobody feels like arguing with him even though many people in this world don't like pepperoni.

On the ride over, Drew begins talking about how "turnt" the party is going to be. Drew is one of those people who tried to fit in to the popular crowd. He went to middle school in a different part of town but was forced to transfer because the bullying was so bad. He wanted to fit in with everyone, which unfortunately isn't possible in high school—at least that's what I've gathered in three years. Everyone has a crowd, and these crowds aren't supposed to mesh. Drew is a stupid son of a bitch sometimes, but finally came to his senses and realized he can't be friends with everyone and became friends with us, which I'm very grateful for.

We arrive fairly quickly, allowing time for three songs in the car ride over: Twenty-One Pilots' "Holding onto You," Twenty-One Pilots' "Car Radio," and Twenty-One Pilots' "Trees," our favorite Twenty-One Pilots song.

Worthington isn't a big city, which I find comforting. It's strange to even try to describe the generic city of Worthington, Ohio. It's primarily middle class, which means there are a lot of two-story homes that surround the roadways. I'm fairly sheltered, which means I haven't seen much besides a few fights in school. Our city motto is, "Worthington Cares," which is ironic in its own right.

But like I said before, everyone knows everyone. Which makes making a mistake miserable, because the person you don't want to know you made the mistake will find out. And this makes for very entertaining school days, causing the only fights I've seen in my young lifetime.

We're forced to park a couple blocks down from Jaret Miller's house because Lindsey told us to. "From personal experience, I would park a decent way up the road because at one of these parties, some drunk kids keyed my car. And I guess it happens if you park super close."

Wise words from Lindsey. To be honest, someone keying my car wouldn't be the worst thing that's happened to me. I'm rocking good ole' reliable. The '93 Saturn whose paint is beginning to peel, and windows won't go down all the way anymore. Jake has been telling me I need to purchase a "real car," but the purpose of a car is to get back and forth to places safely and that's exactly what mine does. I don't need to look good doing it.

We creep up to the door and ring the doorbell. The five of us, standing on the outside of a party. The anticipation runs through my body, along with a touch of excitement and a dash of nerves. I began to hear the music from two houses down but now can make out the songs while standing on the porch—"Pursuit of Happiness" by Kid Cudi. A little different than Twenty-One Pilots on the car ride over.

Lights of all different colors dot the windows, zigzagging almost to the beat of the music. Jaret Miller comes running up and whips the door open, a look of confusion on his face, like he had just seen Darth Vader handing Darth Sidious a fucking lollipop.

"All right, two questions for you guys," he yells. "Who the fuck are you? And why the fuck did you ring the doorbell!?" He needs to yell these two insulting, yet valid questions due to the blaring music in the background, which is too loud for comfort. The smell of his breath catches me off guard: alcohol and Juicy Fruit. Sweat is dripping off his face but yet the gel in his hair is still intact, looking as suave as ever.

Jake, who is in the back, pushes us out of the way and makes his way to the front and starts talking to Jaret Miller. "Hey, what's up, Jaret?" he murmurs out. It was supposed to come out confident but came out slowly and as if he had his mouth filled with tiny slices of pepperoni. He looks like he's in pain. And the rest of us begin to laugh because his face is that funny. Looking like he's trying to find words to say but can't find the right ones. For the first time in his life, Jake is just *almost* speechless. "Yeah, um, Ian invited us. I'm Jake."

The puzzled look remains plastered on Jaret's face. Plus, the look on his face isn't the only thing plastered. He, himself is. His eyes remain fixated on us. "Damn, Ian," he says under his breath, dropping his head, almost as if he knows he's lost. He says it just loud enough for us to hear, but quiet enough to not make a big deal about it.

"All right guys, c'mon in!" He immediately turns his back on us, and without hesitating, we march into the house, one by one, directly following the ring leader. As if my hearing isn't already impaired and my ears aren't damaged by the music, the sight of this party almost blinds me. The sight isn't necessarily shocking, but rather intimidating. The room we walk into is filled with teenagers, shoulder to shoulder with one another. A little tiny hallway which leads to the family room covered with familiar faces, excusing themselves, holding red solo cups in both hands. Everyone seems like they're having fun, or at least acting like they are.

Katie from my pre-calc class this past semester walks by me while I'm waiting in line for the family and squints, like she doesn't recognize who I am. Her hair is lush, which Lindsey told me is a good thing to say to women. I honestly didn't know parties like this were so crowded. I feel like I'm standing in line at a fucking amusement park.

The family room—which we enter a couple minutes later due to the traffic jam—has bright colors moving around the room, similar to the purpose of a disco ball, but the modern-day version. Kids are dancing with each other and on each other, sweat pouring off of each and every one's faces. I've never been grinded on before, but it looks fun. And if I was a betting man, it would feel very good as well. I wouldn't be good at it, though. I'm not good at any stuff like that. It's always been frightening to me. I've always wanted to but could never imagine myself in the situation. Like, where would I put my hands? Or if she even wanted me to do this stuff in the first place. I truly am nervous of making the first move; it scares me to my core.

That's the scariest part in any situation with the opposite gender. Do they want you to do that to them? Do they want you to put your hands on their hips and dance? Do they want you to kiss them? Do they really want to have sex with you? I'm not good at reading these things.

Jaret Miller walks us to the keg which is in the kitchen, the closest room to the family room. The keg has red solo cups stacked in an orderly fashion, like Jaret Miller really put some thought into it. I pick one up and fill it to the top with some beer, not knowing what kind of beer it is. I don't understand the thrill of having your first drink until I actually took a sip. Holding the red solo cup, bringing it up to my lips, and sipping it felt *good*. Like for one night, I may be invincible. The taste is hard to describe. The closest thing to compare it to is having a very bitter drink that is very "crisp."

I look around, feeling eyes on me everywhere I turn. Not just me, but Nick and Drew and Jake and Lindsey as well. The guy looking at us in the corner of the room was Aaron, star of the baseball team. The hot blonde whose eyes are piercing our souls is Maxine, prom queen from this past year. Why her parents named her Maxine is beyond me. Seeing these people makes me upset because they don't know who we are. Maxine doesn't remember me from middle school. She doesn't even remember me from elementary school. Aaron doesn't remember Nick. The star football player, David, doesn't remember Lindsey. Lindsey gave him a blowjob in the bathroom of a Dave 'n' Busters one time. That's how she concluded that she was lesbian.

Although frustrating, people not knowing who we are is refreshing. Because people like us don't get invited to parties. And here we are, a real party. Where anything and everything is allowed. That's how it appears in the movies at least.

Ian sprints in from the family room, meeting us by the keg, sweat pouring down his face. His shirt, which was once light grey, is now a dark shade. His bloodshot eyes open wider when he sees us, which are very wide, "What's up, guys?" he yells. He gives Jake a fist bump.

"What's up, Ian?" Jake yells back. "Look at these guys; they don't even know who we are." With that, Ian takes a quick scan around the party. Realizing how all the eyes are on him and the group of misfits by his side, he turns back to Jake.

"Can you blame them?" he screams. "Don't worry, they'll come around. In the meantime, drink and have fun." And he runs back into the family room, his arms tossed above his head, singing the lyrics to the very entertaining song, "Get Low," which is the one song I imagined they would be playing at a party like this. He seemed happy to see us, which is hard to believe. But even if he isn't, it seemed like he was happy, and that's all that really matters.

I finish my first beer in a couple of minutes and walk over and get myself another, trying to avoid the family room at all costs. I'm not the dancing type. I finish my second beer in a minute or so and get another one. On number 4, I begin feeling different; almost positive I'm wasted at this point. For one, it's my first time drinking, and two, I'm not a big person. So my body can't take much alcohol to begin with.

It's my first time getting drunk or at least what I think is drunk, and the world appears to be changing after every second. Everything seems blurry, but also very clear. The music gets louder, and everyone seems happier. Girls who were once disgusting and horrible looking seem way more attractive.

I also feel lighter. This weight that's been on my shoulders or all of this pressure that I feel about stupid shit has been lifted off. But I also feel heavier, like with every step my balance is challenged a little more than it was before. The lighter I get, the heavier I feel, almost as if I'm doing something wrong.

Lindsey sees me from across the room and waves me over to her. I stumble my way over there and sit next to her. I believe we're in the dining room. A very, very bright light is shining down from a much-too-expensive chandelier. It's gold. Or maybe yellow. I really want to know what color it is, but I don't want to stare at the light too long to find out. Someone told me one time you can become permanently blind if you stare at a light for too long. I'm guessing that's made up, but I don't want to be the one that becomes blind for trying.

I begin playing with Lindsey's hair. She's wearing it a different way tonight. Normally, it's curly but it's straight tonight. Plus, the couch is way more comfortable than a normal couch. There must be a lot of padding underneath that's invisible to the human eye because it truly is the most comfortable thing I've ever sat on. Like, one of those puffy white clouds that float in the sky on a sunny day. Cumulus clouds? Or cumulonimbus? Something like that. One of those.

"Hey, there," Lindsey says, wearing a grin on her face, almost as if she's a proud mom watching her son eat fruit willingly for the first time. "How are you feeling?" She also seems worried, though. Not *too* worried, but enough for me to notice. The type of worried friends get about one another.

"Ya know what, Lindsey?" I say. "I feel terrific. There's nothing on my mind. Zero. Zippo." I smile at her. "I have no fucking clue why there is a couch in this very bright dining room. But have you noticed how comfortable it is?" I say, moving my hand around on the soft material. I'm not quite sure what material it is.

"Well, that's good to hear, but no, I haven't," she says, smiling back. "Do you see Jake over there?" She points toward Jake, who's talking to Jaret Miller and Ian. I don't realize how short and fat he is until I see him with tall and skinny guys like Jaret Miller and Ian. I suppose he's fat because he eats pepperoni slices on the way to parties. Plus, he doesn't work out or run or even walk much. Thinking about the pepperoni slices is making me very hungry. I really want a hamburger or something filling—not pepperoni slices.

"What do you think they are talking about?" I ask her.

"Who the hell knows," she says. "But it can't be good. They're them, and he's him."

It sounds horrible; ridiculing our best friend. But it's the truth. Jake doesn't know what he's getting himself into. He has no idea what he's doing. "Should we do something?" I ask.

She nods and gets up. "You stay here and relax. Watch me work my magic." She winks at me and walks away toward Jake. There I am, sitting on Jaret Miller's couch with a beer in my hand, thinking how I'm sitting on Jaret Miller's couch with a beer in my hand.

Glancing around at the scenery, I soon see Drew talking to Nick in the corner of the kitchen with a bowl of chips sitting on the counter, laughing to one another. Even though I see my best friends talking to each other, the chips are the deciding factor, and I get my drunk ass off Jaret Miller's couch and walk as slowly as possible over to them, doing my best to not cause any disturbances in the flow of the party.

"What's up, guys?" I say to them when I reach 'em. "You guys drinking?"

"What do you think?" Drew asks. "I'm the boy who doesn't drink coffee because it gets me too hyper." He pushes up his glasses after saying this, looking like the cliché nerd in a coming-of-age movie.

I point to Nick. "Are you kidding me?" he asks. "Drinking is for the weak. It's for the people who don't feel good about themselves, so in order to fill whatever sorrow they have in their gut, they drink away whatever pride they don't have."

"That's a no then," I say, slowly dropping my head and taking another sip.

"Why are *you* drinking dude?" Drew asks me. "You do know that is a beer in your hand, right?"

Nick is right when he says drinking is for the weak. Some people drink to make themselves talk to the opposite gender. Some people drink to make the pain go away and forget about their life for a while. And lastly, there are the people who drink to drink. They want to believe they're someone else for a night. These types of people don't believe in the social rank high school provides. Boundaries can be crossed, and groups can be intertwined.

Then there's me; drinking because I don't know what it feels like. Well, *didn't* know what it *felt* like. And in all honestly, I'm not quite sure how I feel about it.

Nick, Drew, and I look across the room and see Lindsey rolling her head. Actually, her whole body. It sort of resembles a sister getting frustrated when her brother is making a mistake. Jake remains in the conversation with Jaret Miller and Ian as I notice Lindsey walking over toward us. Jake points toward Lindsey's butt as she walks away from them…and Jaret Miller laughs.

"So?" I ask Lindsey when she arrives.

She grabs a handful of chips and begins speaking. "Chunky over there is under the impression that those tool bags actually like him. He told me that 'his boys' would like him to be the basketball manager this upcoming year."

"You got to be shitting me," Drew says under his breath. "Doesn't he know that this is how it starts. The athletes in my middle school convinced me to try out for the baseball team and said I was going to make it and become the starting second baseman."

Before he finishes his thought, I question his IQ level for believing in some dumb shit like that. For one, you have to be athletic to play baseball. And two, you have to play baseball in order to play baseball. Drew was neither athletic nor played baseball.

"So, I tried out for the team and I thought I did really well. But it turned out everyone in the tryouts pretended to do really bad, so I thought I was good. The coach was even in on the plan, too. It was some bullshit, man."

Lindsey speaks up before I can. "Drew, even though that is very sad and I'm curious why the fuck someone would do that to another human being, this is Jake we're talking about. Look at him. He's five-

21

foot-five, two hundred something pounds. They're using him. And Jake doesn't know how it feels to be used."

We all know what it feels like to be used besides Jake. Lindsey's ex-girlfriend dated her because she wanted some lemonheads. This was in the seventh grade. Nick believed that his "friends" were his friends because he was cool, but it turned out that they were friends with Nick because Nick bought them season tickets to Ohio State basketball games—he's fucking rich. Drew had that bullshit happen with the baseball team in middle school. And me? The girl I once was interested in told me she was in love with me but then decided that I wasn't good enough for her and started dating my brother.

Jake doesn't know what was going to happen. But we do. We understand. We've lived it. But it turns out Jake is eager to find out. Jake's the person who drinks and pretends that they are someone else for the night. And this moment right now—this epiphany. I discover why Jake brought us to the party.

"Did you know they were looking at your ass when you walked back here?" I ask Lindsey, after minutes pass by of us looking in every direction, people remaining to stare at the unpopular kids sitting on the counters of the kitchen.

"Of course, I did," she says. "Every girl knows when a guy is checking her out. Besides, who wouldn't want to check this piece of ass out? Look at it."

She turns around and Drew, Nick, and I look at it and laugh.

"Damn, Lindsey," Drew says. "If you were straight, I would totally hit that."

As I'm helping my mother down in the basement, I start pitying anyone who has been in my shoes. For one, basements are pointless. No one uses them. Their sole purpose in the world is to store items that families no longer use. Secondly, mothers love basements. This is what makes my job as a child so very difficult.

My mom asked for my help a couple hours ago. Not knowing what I was getting into, I agreed because it felt like the right thing to do. I figured she birthed me, so if I show a pinch of generosity once and a while, I can show that I still, in fact, love her. Not only for the food and shelter and all the necessities, but I love her because she's my mom and I enjoy spending time with her.

My basement looks as follows: a cluster of old, worn-out childhood toys fill the carpet when the stairs end abruptly. No one can walk in my basement due to the horrible mess in which is piled up from wall to wall. There is a very old cabinet that sits on the far wall of the basement which barely remains standing and holds every single board game every created since 1970. We haven't played any board games for years because no one can reach the cabinet. Very poor planning from my mother's part.

When we start cleaning, it goes well. No yelling. No fighting. Just a mom and her child cleaning up a basement which should've been cleaned years prior. But as we dig deeper and make our way toward the middle of the basement, the level of difficulty rises and rises. As does the tension between us.

As a child, I don't understand, not yet anyway. But every toy I have ever played with is buried in this pile of junk. A rattle. A Power Ranger. My mother finds something sentimental about it, whether it's a story or incident. Something lovely or something devastating.

23

She has a reason to not throw the toy away or give to Goodwill. I can't stress enough how frustrating this is.

Five hours pass, and we remain in the basement. My eyes feel like they're going to burst out of my head due to my allergies. When I tell her this, she replies with, "Go get some Benadryl." Little progress has been made and tempers have reached a high. Mom has told me several times, "Ask me if something should be thrown out or not. I have the final say." This only frustrates me more. I strongly try to keep a level head but need to walk upstairs and lay on my bed for a few hours to avoid the conflict that would happen if I was still downstairs.

Mothers love their children; please don't get the wrong impression. My mother loves me just as much as Jake loves high-fructose corn syrup. I appreciate it, I really do. But children grow, and feelings change. What I once liked, I now don't. Children grow up into young adults as parents have already done so. Parents need to know their child's interests change, especially because their feelings once changed and they were once complaining to their own parents about cleaning out basements.

I love my mom. I love how she keeps everything. I love how she asked me to help her clean the basement. I love her so much. So because I love her so much, I go up to my room and lay down. Because if I didn't, we would fight about keeping and not keeping everything. And I don't want to do that.

June 12, 2017

Near the end of school, I've been taking walks. Not necessarily because I enjoy the exercise; I just like looking at everyone and seeing how happy everyone is. I see all different types of people on my walks: children playing tag, male teenagers trying to impress female teenagers, female teenagers trying to seem vulnerable enough to have male teenagers chase after them, families going on walks with their dogs, fathers going on jogs and taking a break from their lives, and old women speed-walking their way to fucking heart failure.

The majority of my walks are short. Long enough for me to start sweating, but short enough to not get tired; the perfect middle ground. One woman, who sits at the corner of the neighborhood, always smiles in my direction and says, "Have a great day."

This woman is always there, not saying anything else to me. She, for the most part, always looks miserable. But for those four words, she looks at me and smiles. I feel very honored and humbled that she does this. I don't know who she is or where she is from.

I reach the corner of the neighborhood and don't see the woman. And for some reason, I get a very bad feeling in my stomach. Something terrible must've happened to her. She is always at the corner of the neighborhood, and today, she isn't. I really hope my gut feeling is wrong. Because it's fascinating how much she meant to me even though I didn't know her. I really care about her. So I'm done taking walks now.

It's safe to say today is a bad day.

June 20, 2017

I have started thinking a lot about Jake a couple weeks ago back at the party. But every time I think about it, it slowly keeps getting worse and worse in my head. I play it back, him talking to Jaret Miller and Ian. Then him leaving the party with Ian rather than us. Thinking of the situation he has put himself in, and not knowing the consequences is difficult for me as a friend. Because I don't want anything to happen to him.

It's Lindsey's birthday, and she shows up in my driveway around four. Drew and Nick eventually arrive around five thirty to spend the night with us. We invite Jake, knowing he will not come. But we figure an invite is necessary because he's been friends with us for this long. I'm pretty sure he's cradling Jaret Miller's balls or something along those lines. Maybe too busy jacking him off, maybe? Whatever it is, he's missing Lindsey's birthday. And if there was one thing Lindsey doesn't tolerate, it's missing her birthday.

We order some pizzas and watch *Criminal Minds*. All four of us have a crush on JJ. We continue to send fan mail to her address and send pictures to be autographed, but she hasn't replied. Not once. Although it hurts, we clearly understand she's a busy woman. I mean, filming a very popular TV show takes up most of a person's time, I suppose. I would be lying if I say I'm not sad, but shit happens. Sometimes your celebrity crush doesn't send back an autograph or her phone number.

We binge watch a couple episodes we've already seen and eat pizza—pepperoni and bacon, Lindsey's favorite. It always makes us shit our brains out the following day, but it's well worth it while it's going down. It's tradition by now. We've been eating the same pizza, watching the same show for the past three years. No matter the day of week or special occasion, we tend to fall back on *Criminal Minds* and pizza because we're not playing it safe, it's fun.

After the pizza is all gone and the episodes without JJ were starting to come on, we begin playing a game where we rank girls from five categories: Ass, titties, face, body, legs. It's based on a ten-point scale, so we rank each feature on a scale from 1–10 and then add up the totals and divide by five at the end to find out the hotness of each girl. It takes a lot of collaboration and communication to agree on the amount of points we give to each feature and a girl's overall score. Why the fuck would we dehumanize women and rank them on a scale of 1–10 simply on their bodies? Because that's what best friends do. They make up some stupid and shitty game and play it for the rest of their lives. Only our game benefits people as well. It helps girls realize how pretty they are. As well as who to date and who not to date. So when I think about it, we're helping our society.

The only rule of the game is we can't grade girls that are exes or girls who we have had relations with. Which isn't a problem with us because none of us have girlfriends, and the only girls we've had relations with were zeros; just being honest. Suzie Humpback from a couple years back might've been in the negatives, but she did give me my first and only blowjob. With a name like Suzie Humpback, I should've known better than to give her some attention. But the blowjob made it all worth it. It was my first orgasm. And I hope and pray young boys across the world get to experience an orgasm orally.

First up is Emma Skates, a golfer at our school. She's a year below us and is very fun and kind. Unfortunately for her, that doesn't help with her score. I give her a six on her butt, seven on tits, nine on face, four on legs, and finally a six on overall body.

"I pretty much agree with those numbers," Lindsey says. "Except I would probably upgrade her legs from a four to an eight. She's got some pretty good hamstrings that lead up to her ass. And while she's golfing, during the middle of her backswing her pants go slightly into her ass crack, which makes both cheeks extremely visible, and it's not bad to look at."

Every group of friends needs a lesbian. It makes life so much easier when she can talk about girls with you. And not like a "She's super pretty" kind of talk. More of a talk where she can use words like *tits* and *ass*.

So overall, we give her a seven on her legs and her total score is a 6.6/10, which isn't half that bad. A solid D. It's quite a simple strategy using just a couple numbers. There's no bullshit algebraic formula that needs to be involved. It's simple and gets to the point. This way we know how hot a girl is. And which girl is out of our league and are just made up fantasies in our head…which happens to be most of them.

We only do a couple girls because Lindsey must run home and spend the late hours of the night with her family. Her mother is an "exotic dancer," which is business talk for stripper, so she works until eleven or twelve every night. I've been told strippers work later, but she must've made a deal with her club because she gets off by midnight every night. Which is good for Lindsey because she needs a woman in her life to tell her about periods and protection. Something her father can't do.

When I first learned about her mother's profession, I was shocked she gets done around eleven. I just assume every drunk dad at least stays up and goes to the strip club around 2:00 or 3:00 a.m. But Lindsey confirmed her mother has a lot of business even though she gets done pretty early. Men who are white trash and pathetic and are in dire need to get a boner go to the strip club at 9:00 p.m. on a Wednesday. And that's what Lindsey's mother is there to do. Her dad is totally comfortable with it too.

Katie Liggins receives a 7.3, Emily Taylor an 8 flat, and Jessica Jenkins gets a 5.6 (underrated, if you ask me). Afterward, Lindsey drives home for the night. It's a good birthday celebration. Never underestimate the little things in life. Hanging out with my friends tonight, time flies. I love when time goes by quickly while spending time with your best friends because it proves how much you love them. You're always doing something productive, even if it isn't. Even if you're ranking girls from a scale from 1–10. And the night is simple and quiet. No distractions or arguments. No late-night parties or alcohol. That's okay. Because I'm with them. And the feeling of being enough for someone is nice.

July 4, 2017

July 4, 2017. America's day. A wonderful time to celebrate the signing of the Declaration of Independence by boozing and watching fireworks light up the sky. Or the sky lighting up the fireworks? I'm not quite sure which one is correct.

My family loves going to the fireworks show that is held at my high school. There are shows across the whole city of Columbus in little, tiny suburbs: Dublin, Gahanna, Hillard. But because my family believes in tradition so strongly, we go to the same one every year. There's nothing like going to see a mediocre firework show in the backyard of your high school.

We arrive around seven thirty. The fireworks start at eight. My dad is the type of dad who parks far away because he doesn't enjoy sitting in traffic on the way out. So we're forced to park in the church that we don't go to, which is located a mile away from the high school. Which I don't feel comfortable with because I bet Jesus is watching us park in one of his safe havens or some shit and we can't even be bothered to go in it.

On the walk over, my brother Chad starts talking about his baseball game he had earlier in the day. He's going to be a junior this upcoming year. He is on this "all-star" baseball team during the summer. Each high school in the city puts three of their players on this team and then plays tournaments throughout the United States. They call it the *Worthington Sluggers*. Supposedly, it's an actual all-star team. But if you ask me and the kids who didn't make the team, it's filled with eight *very* good players and five average players who can afford going to Los Angeles and Chicago and New York City every other weekend. Chad is one of those five.

I would put him on an exception list. He would probably qualify as a candidate for being the worst player on the team. The only reason the coach put him on was because of my dad, who happens to be a lawyer and can afford going to places like LA and New York City. Not only can he pay for my brother, he can pay for half the team to fly to Los Angeles. He's *that* dad who pays the way for their son to achieve excellence.

Not me, though. I constantly tell him I would rather take it up the ass from a very large man with a very large schlong than play baseball. I hate sports. Knowing that one team had to lose while the other team celebrated knowing they are celebrating the other team's failure makes me frustrated and upset so I'd rather not be a part in that.

"Yeah, I didn't get to play today, but my coach promised me I would play tomorrow." This is the bullshit I have to listen to 24–7. Why do I have to put up with it? Because he's part of my family. My dad's part of my family. So is my mom, but I like her. Being part of a family means you have to put up with your family's shit. You must listen to your father because he pays the bills. You have to love your brother because he has to love you back. It's one of the unwritten rules about being family. You don't necessarily have to confess your love to your sibling, but they know. And you know they love you. It's simple.

We arrive to "our spot" at exactly seven fifty-eight, two minutes to spare. I am honestly surprised we aren't late because we tend to be late for everything. My mom used to set the clocks back five minutes from the actual time because she was that desperate. She believed if she saw the clock five minutes before the time it actually was, we would be on time to stuff more often. But this plan failed after we found out that she put the clocks back five minutes. She refused to speak to us for a week after this.

The fireworks are pretty spectacular this year. Some guy named Doug Hoover always announces the fireworks from the football press box. After every year he screams into the microphone and yells, "Wow! What a show! That was the best show in years!!" And this year he's actually right. The finale was incredible. The sky was filled with dozens of different colors making loud BANGS every so often. My favorite type of firework are the ones that don't make loud bangs. They shoot up into the sky making no noise at all, before creating a little sizzling noise as they disappear into thin air. I feel they're under-appreciated so that's why they're my favorite.

It's always funny seeing classmates in the summer when we're out of school. Everything is so awkward, almost as if you're not sup-posed to see them. Even at the city-wide fireworks show, I go to extreme measures to avoid contact with almost everyone from my school.

After the show, we make the mile hike back to our car and make a clean getaway because no one else decides to park in the church parking lot a mile away from the fireworks. My brother keeps com-plaining that his feet hurt from his game today.

"Dude shut the fuck up," I tell him. "You didn't even get to play."

"Watch your language," my mother says to me. "You shouldn't talk to your brother that way." Another unwritten rule of being fam-ily; you cannot cuss your brother out in front of your family. I mean, I guess you can. But you're pretty much writing an invitation for an ass-beating from your mother.

I get a text from Nick when I arrive back to the car saying him and Drew and Lindsey are hanging out at his house if I want to go. I ask my dad if he can drop me off at Nick's house on the way home, and he says yes. Thank God, he says yes. Imagining spending an entire night listening to my dad and my brother talk about baseball is troubling. I just pity my mother because she has to. I'm assuming she'd rather take it up the ass from a very large man with a very long schlong as well than listen to them talk baseball. But I just hope she doesn't tell my dad that because divorce is tricky.

We reach Nick's house shortly after leaving the church's parking lot—he lives very close to the school. My dad and brother are talking about how their season is going, and I quickly open the door and close it behind me, saying goodbye to my mom. I walk to the door, up the gravel sidewalk, which is very curvy, but it's rude to walk through someone's front yard, only to be welcomed by a new mat laying directly before you step into the house. It has the faces of Tyler Joseph and Josh Dun, the band members of the band Twenty-One Pilots.

Tyler Joseph, the lead singer is from our town. Sometimes he occasionally pops up once in a while in Worthington, and everyone loses their shit. Nick is *obsessed* with them. He's been to at least ten concerts, knows all their songs, and has every piece of Twenty-One pilots' memorabilia imaginable. His obsession started when he found out that his mother taught Tyler Joseph in like third grade or something like that. So he believes because his mom taught him, he's best friends with him. It makes sense when I think about it. Then I think harder and it doesn't.

I walk down to the basement and spot Nick, Drew, and Lindsey sitting on the couch. Nick's parents always cover the couches and chairs with plastic wrap so in the rare occasion of a spill, nothing gets on their precious sofas. It made sense when we were like six, but we've grown out of the age of spilling shit. His basement is always freezing and immediately makes my nipples hard, pinching out of my shirt.

Lindsey sees me walk down the steps. "Nice nipples," she says.

They are playing NBA 2K when I notice the TV, which is kind of ironic because we're terrible at sports. Nick is playing Lindsey. Drew's just admiring the show which is occurring before him. Nick is the Pelicans and Lindsey is the Kings. I honestly can't say if either of those teams are good or not, but I think one of them has LeBron James.

"You have to say that every time I come down here?" I ask. I have very sensitive nipples that get hard very quickly, which causes me to be very cautious when I run because they easily chafe. Luckily for me, I don't run that often. Not only lucky for me, but my nipples as well.

"How were the fireworks tonight?" Lindsey asks me. "Let me guess, the best show ever?"

I laugh. "Best one in years," I say jokingly. "What did you guys do all night? You go to the fireworks?"

"No, sir, we did not," Drew answers. "First of all, you should've known the answer to that question due to Lindsey's question.

Secondly, we asked Jake if he wanted to go but he said he already had plans with Jaret Miller and Ian, so we decided we had plans as well."

"Oh yeah?" I say. "And what were these plans?"

"Sit here. Talk to one another. Experience life."

And I can't argue with that logic. These guys are all I have. And I can't believe I was wasting time with my family rather than hanging out with them. The fireworks were really good though. It's a guilty pleasure of mine—fireworks. At least it isn't porn of feet or something weird like that.

I can't get myself to watch porn to be honest. Pornography is usually a seventeen-year-old's best friend…every other night at least. Maybe twice a day. But not me. I watched it once, and I couldn't stop thinking these men and women were once children. And these children had mothers and fathers. And how could these mothers and fathers let their children enter the pornography business? And what made these once cute children want to turn into gross, disgusting people who had sex with one another for a living? Were these people sexually harassed as children or were they tormented by their siblings? Or did they even have siblings? I don't know. Every question led to another question for me which is why I don't watch it. I honestly don't even masturbate that often. Only days when it's extremely necessary. Everyone has days like that.

I look up to the TV and see Lindsey is beating Nick in 2K, and I don't even really care. Can't care less to be honest. I'm just there, in the freezing cold basement, with my nipples popping out of my shirt, and no one seems to care. I just need to remember never to take a date down here into Nick's basement, that would be very embarrassing.

July 5, 2017

Before I know it, the clock reads midnight and I'm still sitting on the plastic-wrapped couch next to Drew and Lindsey. Drew smells horribly. And I don't know why because he's never smelled like this before. "Why do you smell this bad?" I ask him. Friends can ask friends these types of questions.

"I'm sweating," he responds quickly, not looking away from the T.V.

"It's below zero," I say.

"Indeed, it is. But you're not playing this game, which is tormenting and horrible and causes people to sweat like this."

Nick has gone up to bed, even though it's his house. He trusts us enough to not break anything, so he went to bed. I need to go soon too. I've had a long day doing nothing except sitting on couches and walking a total of two miles. It's a tough life I live.

I tell Drew and Lindsey, who are still playing 2K, that I am leaving so I get up and say goodbye to Nick's parents, who are half asleep watching TLC in their family room. Before walking out the door, I remember my parents dropped me off, so I can't leave unless someone takes me home, so I go back downstairs to see if Drew or Lindsey can take me home. One of the most awkward things in the world is when you have already said goodbye to someone and then you see them again. It happens in grocery stores all the time. You talk to someone for a while and you say, "It was great to see you!" and then they say, "It was great to see you too!" and you guys both go your separate ways and then see each other at least three more times in different aisles.

I ask Drew if he can give me a ride and he says, "I guess so," so he takes me home. We don't talk about much. But his car smells like air freshener, which overruns the stench beneath his armpits, so it's quite pleasant.

34

July 9, 2017

My city has just built a place called IKEA, which is a furniture store on steroids. The original one was built in Sweden which is pretty crazy to think about; how an idea can travel across the world.

Nick and I go at four, which isn't a bad time to go because all the crazy moms aren't there quite yet. Rush hour is around five or six when people get off work and people's wives go and explore the store like it's fucking Disney World. I honestly think going to IKEA is some people's vacation for the summer.

IKEA only has two floors, but they're huge. The upstairs is where people usually tend to go first because of the food court. There aren't too many options, so people won't get overwhelmed, but enough so people have a nice variety to choose from. People can also become an IKEA family member which, once signed up, can provide you free complimentary coffee or tea every day. This also allows IKEA to send you emails every minute of every day. I've found out the hard way.

There are also shopping opportunities on the second floor. On the floor, there are arrows which are lit up by a hanging overhead projector that lead the way and tells the customers where to go. The furniture is placed in different locations around the second floor and is put in these little tiny rooms which are built to show how people furnish certain rooms. Each piece of furniture has a number, so you must remember the number and then go downstairs and pick it up from the first floor. All of the shit is stocked on the first floor in like a big warehouse-looking room.

Not only is the warehouse on the first floor, but little items are for sale down there as well, like picture frames or cubes to put in dressers. Everything a woman would like, it can be found on the first floor. I guess everything women like can be found on the second floor too. But the first floor is more artsy-type stuff. They have EVERYTHING there, ranging from whole fucking kitchens to little tiny screws and tools. I'm not saying men don't enjoy the store, but typically it's not a man's dream to build an "ideal family room."

I'm part of the minority that does, though. I'll admit, it makes me excited to get out of the house and get my own apartment. Nick agrees with me. It makes me excited to get a girlfriend and settle down and start a family. It presents hope, which a teenager like me can really use. IKEA gave me hope.

Walking around the store is funny because I see couples holding hands and pointing to this and that, and I'm walking alongside Nick. These couples have their hopes and dreams mapped out in their heads. The look of terror on the boys faces, knowing that one day they are going to come back and buy this stuff for their girlfriend or wife.

But I want that too. I want the look of terror on my face. I want to show someone that I can buy them stuff from IKEA. I'm going to bring a girl here and we will be pointing to mattresses and desks and lamps and chairs and couches. I know it. Not until I'm financially stable and know I'm going to marry this girl. Not every girl deserves a trip to IKEA with me. Only *the One*.

Knowing I will soon regret it, I decide to call Jake and see what he is doing tonight. But when he answers, "Probably hanging with Jaret and Ian," I almost gag and kill myself. After not responding, he texts me and says I can come over and hang out with them. I think it will be fun to see Jake again and talk about how things are going, especially not hearing from him all summer.

I show up at his house around eight thirty. It's just like old times. I walk right in the door; his mom and dad greet me like they saw me yesterday. They say hi and then go back to whatever they were doing. I think his dad is playing solitaire and his mom is knitting—the horrifying origin of Jake.

Quickly, I walk up to Jake's room to see him sitting on his bed, accompanied by Jaret Miller drinking some beer, Natty Light to be precise.

"What up, man?" Jake says to me. "Long time no see."

"Yeah," I say, looking down at the ground, trying my best to avoid eye contact with either of them. "How you been?"

"Splendid," Jake answers. "Living the good life my man. Drinking and living, ya know?"

Drinking and living? What the fuck? "Yeah, I guess I know what you mean," I say. "Hey, Jaret."

I hesitantly look up to see Jaret Miller sitting on Jake's bed, fairly similar to how I used to sit on his bed. "Sup, guy," he responds. I truly don't know how it's physically possible to become more of a dick. I'm not quite sure how he should've responded, but his demeanor just screams dickhole.

"What's the plan tonight?" I ask. "I mean, do you want to play some *Call of Duty* or something? It'll be just like old times, man."

Jake laughs. "For as fun as that sounds, we're going out tonight. We're gonna go downtown to a bar called Bulls. And you are coming with us." He points at me, yet I still think he's pointing at someone else. The fat and chubby know-it-all who played *Call of Duty* on a Monday has turned into a fat, chubby know-it-all who goes to bars on Monday nights. What went wrong in his life that he is considering going to a bar on a Monday?

I laugh. Openly laugh. I can't resist. "Are you shitting me, dude? Are you *shitting* me? In case you haven't noticed, we haven't talked in over a month. I don't drink. Plus, I don't even talk to this douche over here. He fucking sucks."

Jaret Miller just nods, completely agreeing that he fucking sucks.

"I respect all of that," Jake says. "And I know that I haven't been a good friend to you. But we're going to have fun tonight, I promise. You need to let loose a little bit. You have to let the night control you once in a while and not let yourself control the night."

I'm a pretty stubborn fella. When I don't want to do something, typically I stand my ground. I don't do anything that feels uncomfortable. But this is Jake. If this is what needs to be done to spend time with my best friend, it's an easy yes. Even though I'm more than likely not going to enjoy myself, Jake will enjoy himself, and friends realize when they're making an effort.

So he talks me into going out to party with him and Jaret Miller. We take an Uber to this place called Bulls, which is a bar downtown. Ubers are very uncomfortable. Sitting in the backseat, trusting someone who probably shouldn't be trusted is beyond dumb. But I figured if I'm going to a bar on a Monday, I might as well do other dumb shit, so an Uber is the move for the night.

The Uber driver, Eric, a fat white guy who showed us his *Yu-Gi-Oh!* collection, drops us off directly in front of the bar. We walk up and get in line behind some girls. I notice the bouncer is making people show him their IDs and I begin freaking out. Jake hands me a Pokémon card and tells me to show the bouncer this and he will let me through.

Believe it or not, the bouncer actually lets me go into the bar with a Pokémon card. To be fair it was Mewtwo, the best Pokémon to ever exist in the Pokémon land, but still. He lets me in with a fucking Pokémon card. The girls before us don't show him anything and the man gave them a smirk and waved them in, like they're regulars, which they probably are. But I'm in no position to judge. If you're a girl in the twenty-first century and you want to go to a party, you're in. No if's or but's. Just show a little cleavage, which these girls do.

We walk in the bar to see flashing lights of all different colors and sexual dancing on the dance floor. The music is dangerously loud and is already damaging my eardrums, probably permanently. It's the same exact scene I witnessed walking into Jaret Miller's party in the beginning of summer, but just escalated: louder music, brighter colors, and way more people on the dance floor. It's a Monday night, and this bar is packed.

"All right, boys!" Jaret Miller yells. "The first one is on me tonight!" He then walks away to a counter that is directly in the middle of the room. I see the bartender look at him, and I begin to get worried that he won't get him any drinks. The bartender quickly daps him up and lays out three tiny shot glasses. He then pours this clear liquid into all three of them, just filling them up without spilling any, the perfect bartender.

He comes walking back, handing us the little glass cups and says, "Here's to one hell of a night."

Jake jumps in, "Bro, do the fucking toast!"

Jaret Miller nods several times, understanding what he's asking. "My bad dude. My bad." He then raises his glass. When Jake follows, I do the same. "To wood ships, and good ships, the ships that sail the sea. But the best ships are friend ships...and may the always be."

Jake screams, "Hell yes!" over the loud music, and we tilt our heads back and force the alcohol into our mouths. I forgot how bad alcohol was since that first night of summer when I had a couple beers at Jaret Miller's party. All alcohol is disgusting. But it isn't supposed to taste good. It's supposed to get you drunk—that's its sole purpose.

I walk over to the bar alongside Jake. He buys us a pitcher of beer and says, "This one is on me. Thanks for coming." Jake hands me a cup and pours beer into it, the stench, smelling horribly. I drink it and then he pours me another one. Then I drink that one and he pours me another. Soon enough, Jake buys another pitcher and I'm five or six beers deep, and I need to go to the bathroom. Like, bad.

I haven't quite mastered the art of drinking yet. I've only drank twice in my life, and there's no sipping for me. The taste of alcohol is so goddamn bad I have to chug it if I'm going to drink it at all.

While I'm walking toward the bathroom, I see a group of girls sitting on a circular round couch thing that looks so comfortable. It's an odd feeling that flows through my body. I'm pretty sure I'm drunk for the first time in my young life, compared to Jaret Miller's house where I felt weird. I've heard people call this *tipsy*. Right before you get drunk, you get "tipsy," which I concluded I was after talking to Lindsey about it and after feeling the feeling I'm feeling, which is a lot weirder than the feeling I felt at Jaret Miller's.

Seventeen years young, and I am officially drunk. It's an odd feeling. And by odd, I mean truly fantastic. It's almost as if nothing can defeat you. You can't give two shits about what people are thinking of you and what you're doing. You become a different person when you're drunk.

So for some peculiar reason, I decide to walk over to these beautiful girls sitting on a very comfy-looking couch. Nothing on my mind except their beauty and how comfy this fucking couch looks; I can't get over it. With confidence running through my veins, I pop a squat next to the prettiest girl of the bunch, the last one on the couch.

"Can I help you?" one of the girls says. It comes from one of the girls in the middle. I see every head turned toward me, assuming the look of disgust rests on each of their faces. Even though I can't see their faces because of the darkness of the bar, I can sense it. It's probably valid because I definitely invited myself, but at least act like you're a decent human being.

"Well," I start, "I was drinking beer with my friend Jake, well, ex-friend. He kind of abandoned me for this kid who goes to our school named Jaret Miller. I didn't even want to be here, but he pretty much kidnapped me and threw me in a car with him *unwillingly*." I'm stretching the truth just a tad bit.

"But now I'm here drinking liquids I don't normally consume. And I really needed to go to the bathroom, so I started walking toward the bathroom and I saw this incredible looking couch, or maybe a sofa, I don't know what they're called, but I had to sit on it."

I hear cackling and laughter and see everyone from the couch/sofa leave in an instant. Except the girl I'm sitting next to. She seems alarmed, like something with me isn't clicking the way it should. This girl might be actually worried about me, a stranger who she's never met before.

"Are you okay?" she asks me, moving closer now so our legs are almost touching. Her leg isn't big or small. But who cares the size, it's almost touching mine.

"Your friends left," I say, pointing at them while they walk away. "And this couch is not as comfortable as it seemed."

She chuckles. Not quite a laugh, but a slight smile comes across her face. "They're not my friends. They're just some girls I go to school with."

"You are truly stunning." That's the beer talking. What the fuck am I saying? "The way your hair is tucked behind your ear is beautiful." There was only one side of her head with hair tucked behind her ear. The other side had hair flowing down, covering the rest of her face. A style that is very underappreciated and is very beautiful.

"Awe, you're too sweet," she says, blushing. She probably gets that a lot so that's the comment she always says back. "Tell me more about this ex-friend of yours." She seems like she means what she says. She honestly seems concerned about me. Actually, not concerned, but interested, like, she's trying to get to know me. I try to speak but the overwhelming feeling of pee starting to trickle out of my penis makes me jump off the overrated couch sofa.

"Please excuse me," I say. "I really have to go to the bathroom."

"I'll be here."

I fast-walk to the bathroom, quickly find the nearest urinal and pee the best pee I've ever peed. The overwhelming sensation of purity and joy runs through my veins. It's like having your first orgasm or something, so clear and so pure. The dude next to me even tells me to "stop moaning," but I have to moan. That's how good of a piss it is.

I don't wash my hands, like most men do, and walk back to the sofa with the cute girl on it. She's still there!

"Hey, you're still here."

"I told you I'll be here," she says, smiling. "How was your pee?"

"Unbelievable," I answer, sitting back down next to her, legs touching this time. "I really like your dress." A light blue dress that goes down just above the knees, little tiny pieces of watermelon sprinkled all over it.

"Oh yeah, thanks. I believe watermelon is the most underrated fruit. Everyone always talks about apples and bananas, but I freaking love watermelon."

I smile. Not just that small talk smile you're forced to do while talking to a family friend or some shit, but a real smile. I don't remember the last time I've smiled without Nick, Drew, Lindsey, and Jake. "I could not agree more, it's extremely underrated. I like to think of watermelons as people, ya know?"

"Elaborate," she says, tilting her head, looking at me. Her eyes are blue and big. Not staring into my soul, but just staring at me. It's gentle and warm, a feeling I've never noticed before in eyes. I didn't know eyes could be so warm.

"I mean, it's like you just said, people always eat apples and bananas. Girls always go for the Jaret Miller type. Girls can't resist someone who is athletic and stupid. It's like they're driven to be attracted to people like that. People like Jaret Miller are the apples and bananas. And girls can never get enough fucking apples and bananas."

The music is still blaring in the background, but becomes less and less apparent as I continue talking to this girl. All my attention is on her. "So, what are melons like? That is what we're doing right, comparing delicious snacks to men?"

"We're the non-athletic type. The type that doesn't mind staying in on a weekend and getting eight hours of sleep. The type that loves hanging out with their friends doing nothing but eating pizza and watching *Criminal Minds*. The type that doesn't really care going unnoticed. That's what people like Jaret Miller crave—attention. They want to be prom king. They want to be the one who sleeps with all the girls in school. They care about shit that doesn't need to be cared about." I'm rambling, but it's nice to talk to her.

She nods. "I think I'm getting this ridiculous, yet very truthful, metaphor. Girls are tricky sometimes. All we really want is someone that will take care of us at the end of the night. We want someone to hold us and talk to us. We just want someone that cares, ya know?"

"Yes, I completely understand. But until that comes, all of you want some sexy guy that can break wood on his abs or some guy that can fuck you and has experience fucking girls. It seems like girls only want a relationship when they're tired of sleeping around with boys. They want to be comforted after that. They don't want to have meaningful sex with someone they love until they have half of the male's populations dicks up in them." I think I've gone too far. "Sorry."

"Don't apologize," she says. "You're absolutely right. Side note—how drunk are you?" She's caught off guard from my previous statement. "You're pretty new at this aren't you?"

"Extremely," I answer, having the sudden urge to already pee again. "I've only drank one other time and that was in the beginning of summer and I didn't really get drunk, I just felt a little off. But right now, I can probably defeat the entire Empire by myself."

She giggles, not just a normal giggle, but a flirtatious one. At least I take it as flirtatious. She rests her hand on my leg, "I'm not quite sure what's worse; those words really came out of your mouth or I understood what you were talking about."

Losing my breath over this girl, I burst out, "What's your name?" suddenly realizing that I haven't asked for her name before just now.

She smiles before saying, "Jordyn Marie Wright."

And what a beautiful name it is.

July 12, 2017

So there I am, getting girl advice from two freaks and a lesbian, who I suppose can also be classified as a freak. I tell Drew, Nick, and Lindsey about Jordyn, the girl I met in the bar a couple nights ago. At first, they were frustrated with me for going to the bar with Jake. When they finally get over it, they think I am making her up because I tell them she understood my Star Wars reference. When I start giving them more details about her like the color of her eyes and how beautiful she was and what her family was like, they think I am officially crazy.

When I finally pinky swear to them she is not a fictional character I made up in one of my stories I have to write for a summer assignment, they decide to enlighten me on the feminine mind, and what an interesting mind it is.

Drew starts off by telling me it would be a good idea to text her, "Hey," with one of those smirky face emojis. But Lindsey then tells me I shouldn't text her because I should let her make the first move. I tell her that idea was borderline impossible because she gave me her number and I didn't give her mine. Nick finishes by saying the worst idea of all, "Don't text her." He tells me not to do anything because he doesn't want me to get hurt. Part of me understands what he says, but another part of me hates him for it. A pretty girl possibly kind of low-key showed affection toward me, and he doesn't want me to do anything about it.

"Are you kidding me, man?" I ask him. "This girl might like *me*, and you don't want me to shoot my fucking shot? What kind of friend are you?"

"Dude, I'm sorry," he says. "But I don't want you to get hurt over some girl that you just met. I mean, if you like her, go for it, but please don't come crying back to us wanting half of my pizza on a Thursday night when she doesn't text you back."

I understand what he's saying. It makes sense. How can a good-looking girl like Jordyn Marie Wright have a crush on a fucking watermelon? But being the dumb guy that I am, I decide to text her, knowing the potential risks it may cause.

For real, I'm not good at making friends. But Jordyn…it seemed easy. When we had that conversation at the bar, which only ended because Jake was throwing up in the bathroom and had to be airlifted out of there, it seemed natural. Like, I wasn't even myself. I forgot about everything when I began talking to her, like it was something that happened for a reason.

"So, what did you go with?" Lindsey asks, a couple minutes later after I text her. "What'd you say? Something sexy? Something subtle? Something that is very subtly sexy? Give us all the details?"

"I asked her how her twin sister's soccer game went last night. That's okay, right?"

Jordyn answers quickly:

Ugh, so boring. Who is this by the way?

We all start laughing like crazy.

It's Watermelon…

…

Oh, hey Melon! Thanks for asking! How are you?

"Look at that!" Lindsey screams. "You've got her ass on that goddamn fishing line! Reel her in baby!"

"Relax, dummy. She asked me how I was. She didn't ask me out."

I respond:

> I'm grand thanks ☺ Hey I have a question.
> How would you like to go see a movie with me
> tomorrow night? My treat ☺

"Okay, way to be straightforward, but please relax on the smiley faces," Nick says. "It's cool to do with us because we know you so well, but it could freak her out." Absolutely right. Plus, I asked her out too fucking quick. No one asks someone out after three text messages.

She answers a couple minutes later:

> I can't tomorrow, sorry ☹ Have plans with
> the bf. What about the day after tomorrow? I'll
> buy the popcorn.

"Bf?" Drew asks. "Best friend?"

"Probably boyfriend," Lindsey says. "I mean if she's as great as *watermelon* says she is—and I really dislike the whole watermelon metaphor—she has to have a boyfriend."

Disappointedly, I answer:

> Oh, no worries! Have fun with the best
> friend!

"Real fucking sly man! Real fucking sly!" Nick yells.

Then my phone vibrates, and I can't help myself but look at it as quick as possible. I reach for it in my pocket and read:

> Bf meaning boyfriend, Melon, haha

How could she not mention she has a boyfriend? That's a pretty big detail to leave out. I mean, she told me everything else about her life. Where she was from (Ada, Ohio), how many siblings she has (three), favorite movie (*Perks of Being a Wallflower*), favorite book

(*An Abundance of Katherines*). And there were so many more questions she had answers to: favorite color, drink, vacation spot, sport, candy, food, TV show, article of clothing. Everything I asked, she had answers for. I knew everything about her after one amazing night. Except her relationship status. A real, human, living boyfriend.

"It's all good man," Nick says. "Soccer has goalies; doesn't mean you can't score."

And I guess that's true. But I'm really not looking to score. She's amazing and not the hookup type. I'm not the hookup type. I'm nerdy, skinny, and a joke. She's smart, fit, and amazing. And the worst part is, she has a boyfriend.

July 14, 2017

She wants me to pick her up around seven thirty, but I tell her not until eight because I have chores to finish up. I don't have any chores. The movie doesn't start until eight thirty and what kind of person wants to sit in a movie theatre for forty-five minutes to watch those stupid advertisements about Trojan condoms or Axe deodorant or whatever? Not me. So I put my foot down and say eight.

After compromising, we settle on the pickup time—seven thirty. How can I deny spending extra time with her? I don't arrive at seven twenty-nine or seven thirty-one, precisely seven thirty, trying my best to please her. I hope she notices.

Her house is pretty on the outside. It's a two-story house with TWO garages. A beautiful-looking garden surrounds the walkway, twisting and turning from the driveway, leading up to the front door. It sounds very cliché and stereotypical, but it's a very middle-class home.

I debate on the proper way to present myself to her. Is walking to the door too cliché? Is texting her "I'm here" too millennial? Settling on a decent middle ground, I honk the horn of my '93 Saturn, like the gentleman that I am at seven thirty-one. I wait patiently for her to come out, looking as beautiful as ever. At seven thirty-two, she comes running out, wearing black flip-flops, toenails painted this pretty turquoise color, with a romper covering everything else. How do I know what a fucking romper is? Now that, is a very good question.

I quickly get out and run around the car to open her door.

"Oh wow!" she gasps. "First honking the horn, now opening my door. I think I'm in love." No, I'm in love.

"Shut up," I say sarcastically. Wow, I'm in love.

I start driving as she begins to speak. "Okay. So. Although this movie looks good, my stomach is being a nuisance, so we must stop and get some grub *por favor.*"

I groan. "Ugh, are you kidding me, Jordyn Marie?"

"I know, I know. My sincere apologies, but a growing girl's gotta eat."

"I suppose so. There's a Chipotle next to the theatre so we can get ourselves a big, fat burrito, and take it in the movie."

"Sounds dope!" she yells.

"Dope?"

"Yes, D-O-P-E. Dope.

"And that means?"

"Wow, you're so uneducated. You need to stop watching *Criminal Minds* and *Star Wars* and start living. *Dope* means cool."

"Why can't I just say, 'cool'?"

"Cuz. *Dope* is doper."

She has a point. But I may just stick with *cool* for now.

The conversation runs swimmingly. I don't make a fool of myself during the drive, and she continues to talk to me—two very good signs this is going well. Surprised is an understatement.

We order our burritos pretty quickly and walk in the movie theatre at seven fifty-eight. How do I know the exact time we walk in the movie theatre? Well, I ask Jordyn what time it is when we walk in, and she says seven fifty-eight.

I have to carry her burrito through the ticket line because "Rompers don't have pockets, Melon." Then, I counter and say some of my mom's rompers have pockets, and she proceeds to mock me because I actually know some of my mom's rompers have pockets. I dug my own grave on that one.

We take our seats in theatre 18 to watch *Baby Driver,* an action-packed but also supposed to be funny movie that stars the one and only Ansel Elgort. He is also in this movie called *The Fault in Our Stars* according to Jordyn. Which is a "tragic movie that centers around teenage love and heartbreak that is based on the bestselling novel by John Green. Who happens to be my favorite author." I know that's her favorite author. I just didn't know that movie/book. Sounds sad if you ask me.

The movie trailers start, and I reach into my pockets and pull out both of our burritos, which are both surprisingly still warm. I hand her the one that has the giant *V* marked on it for "vegetarian."

"I still can't believe you're a vegetarian, you communist," I whisper to her softly.

"Oh really? You've never heard and or used the word *dope*, Melon. I think I win this battle and will win the war when that war comes." We then, tap our burritos against one another's and begin eating.

There is a huge leather armrest right in the middle of us that can easily be folded up, so we can "cuddle," but she has a boyfriend. Honestly, even if she didn't, I wouldn't want to snuggle with her on the first date. I am no whore.

We talk through the movie trailers, rating them on a scale of 1–20. Jordyn doesn't believe in scales that go from 1–10 because "Why would I rate something an 7.5/10 when I can rate it a 15/20?" Part of me understands, but the other 99 percent of me does not.

Soft chattering turns to utter silence when the movie starts. When I watch a movie, I don't like to be bothered, and Jordyn feels the same. She wants to focus all her attention on the film. We don't say one word to each other the whole, entire movie. And that is all right. Because I am sitting next to the most beautiful girl in the world and no one else is...except the goth girl who is sitting on the other side of her. She is too.

July 15, 2017

Last night, while being one of the best nights of my life, was also one of the worst. I had found *The One* but couldn't ask her to be my girlfriend because she has a boyfriend. I went over to Nick's house earlier in the day to watch some *Criminal Minds* episodes and chill. This is not to be confused with "Netflix and chill," which supposedly means having sex while Netflix is on in the background. I mean, watching *Criminal Minds* while sitting on the couch next to Nick. But trust me, no sex is involved.

I'm not quite sure how I've concluded that she's *The One*. Someone doesn't just wake up one day and decide the person they're hanging out with is *The One*. It should develop over time and not over a two-hour movie. At the end of the day, though, I suppose there's not a lot of choice in the matter. You're either lucky enough to find it or spend too much time thinking about how you can't find it.

I was texting Jordyn throughout the day, but nothing major. Small talk: How her day was going, what she was doing, how she's feeling. Pretty much a text conversation between middle schoolers who have crushes on each other.

> Boy: *Hey.*
> Girl: *Hey.*
> Boy: *How's it going*
> Girl: *Good, U?*
> Boy: *Good. Whatcha doing?*
> Girl: *Nmu?*
> Boy: *Same.*

Some shit like that. But worded better, and in more of an adult way. Better diction, like "What are you doing?" Rather than "Whatcha doing?" That makes all the difference.

Nick had told me him and Lindsey were going to the bowling alley later tonight if I wanted to go. Ever since we were kids, Lindsey had this obsession about going to the bowling alley. "Something about wearing other people's shoes turns me on," I believe was her exact quote.

I said yes, of course, because I wanted to do something with them and not think about Jordyn. Besides, I don't want to be one of those guys that falls for a girl and thinks about them 24-7. I've seen those people. And those people suck big fucking nuts.

Around 7:00, I hear a gay little car horn in my driveway, which was the gay little car horn of Nick's car. When I say gay, I clearly don't mean it in a bad way, or in a literal sense of the word. Clearly, car horns cannot be gay. I mean, it was a high-pitched horn that gave me the fruity feeling that gay people have. And I'm allowed to judge like this due to the fact that I have a lesbian friend. It lets you off the hook on shit like that.

I walk out the door and yell goodbye to my mother. My dad and brother are in Las Vegas for a baseball tournament, so it's just me and the mom for a couple days. I see Nick in the driver's seat with Lindsey next to him, her bare feet on the dashboard.

"Damn, Lindsey, can you put your jacked-up feet somewhere else?" I yell at her, jogging toward the car, unaware that the windows were open. I shouldn't have said anything because when I enter the car, she climbs in the backseat and puts her feet directly in my face where I can smell the horrible smell of feet, and maybe tuna. She has a freckle on the bottom of her foot that I never noticed before.

I suddenly freak out and attempt to push her feet and legs off of me. To no advantage though due to Lindsey's freakishly strong lower body. Her legs are like fucking tree trunks. I keep trying, but when I finally decide that my fate is determined, and I'm going to die by the stench of Lindsey's feet, I give up and tap. Lindsey respects my tap-out and takes her legs off me and climbs back in the passenger seat. I look out the window and notice we are still sitting in my driveway.

"Why the hell aren't we moving?" I ask Nick.

Nick starts laughing. Really laughing. "Lindsey just made you her bitch man!" he yells out at the top of his lungs, continuing to laugh. "And you thought I *wasn't* going to get that on video?"

Lindsey starts to laugh now. Nick, with a smile on his face, reaches his hand in the backseat and begins waving his phone directly in front of my face.

"It's not my fault she has fucking legs as strong as a fucking gravitation pull!" I yell, still smelling the scent of Lindsey's feet. Seriously. Why do her feet smell like tuna?

"What can I say?" She says. "Girls love a big ass and strong legs. Makes us great in bed."

"How does having strong legs and a big ass make you better in bed?" I ask.

She looks at me with a puzzled look. At this point, Nick starts driving and put a Twenty-One Pilots song that blares through the speakers, giving me the beginning state of a headache. That, and the wrestling match I just took part in.

"We really need to get you laid," she says to me. "Honest to god. We need your penis inside a girl's vagina as soon as possible."

"Dude?" I say, looking at her in disbelief. Her word choice was interesting, leaving an extremely vivid picture in my mind that I don't want there. "You have to say that?"

"I'm serious, man! You're a great guy, and you deserve to bone someone! You deserve at least that!"

Bone someone? Do I want to bone Jordyn? It sounds like that would hurt her.

I really want to have sex with Jordyn. To be honest, I've thought about it a lot. But I can't picture myself doing that. I can't see myself laying naked beside her. I can't see myself kissing her neck, rubbing my hands against her back. I can't see myself, like Lindsey said, "putting my penis inside her vagina." I would like to, though. Sex just makes things weird between people. Sex leads to a lot of things that could lead to a lot of other things which can lead to a lot of negative outcomes, and I'm not ready for that yet. There's more bad that can come out of sex than good. So I'm going to stay away from it for a little longer.

I want to kiss her on the cheek. I want to call her when she's driving home from school to ask her how her day was. I want to lay in bed beside her while she closes her eyes to me rubbing my fingers through her hair. I want all the little romantic moments that people don't do enough of. I guarantee you Jordyn's boyfriend doesn't look forward to calling her as much as I would. He doesn't smile every time he hears her speak. The words coming off her tongue, out of her mouth like she's reading a poem. I swear I can watch her speak all day because watching her lips move is like watching a miracle happen right before your eyes.

But I'm not one of those people that fall for a girl and thinks about them 24-7.

We pull in the parking lot, which is surprisingly almost full, and walk in. Star Lanes is a bowling alley where you can bowl and play games. It is filled with the sounds of balls knocking pins down and multiple birthday parties with screaming children wanting a piece of cake. There're twenty lanes to bowl, and on a common day, half of those are filled with teenagers illegally purchasing alcohol and legally eating pizza.

We buy our tickets, which are pretty expensive, and go and grab our bowling shoes. You can see Lindsey's face brighten up as she orders her shoes from the creepy man behind the counter. He has something stuck in his mustache, which I tell him about, motioning to my own lip. He picks up on what I'm doing and quickly dispatches of the random piece of food he was saving for later. I would hope someone would tell me I had a piece of food stuck on my face, so I did him a favor.

We go and sit in the chairs of lane 19. Lindsey slides her feet out of her flip flops and puts her bare feet inside the red-and-white bowling shoes. Exhibit A on why her feet smell like tuna.

"I can't believe what I just witnessed," Nick says, a look of amazement plastered on his face. "I mean, I can't believe it. I just saw a girl put her bare feet inside a pair of hundred-year-old bowling shoes. I mean, I figured you had socks or something in your purse."

"You mean feet prison?" yells Lindsey. "I will not allow my feet to be trapped inside of socks. Are you kidding?"

I smile, and it's not because I love bowling. It's because of this argument that's pointless. Pointless conversations are a catalyst for best friends to remain best friends. It's this stuff you can't forget about when you become old and brittle.

I'm the first one to bowl, beginning with two gutter balls. Bad gutter balls too. I don't think they made it halfway down the lane before going into the gutter. I tried the spinning technique, which obviously failed.

Nick is after me, and he walks up and says, "Watch this," as if calling his own homerun on the very next pitch. I only know this because my brother tried it one time and then struck out in three pitches.

He throws his arm back aggressively, holding the ball, and swings it forward, releasing the ball quickly. The ball goes spiraling down the center of the lane and crashes into the pins, knocking all ten over.

He looks back at us, lifts his shirt, and smacks his stomach, yelling, "Wooooo!"

"What the fuck is that celebration?" I say, laughing.

"It's mine. Just made it up. Like it?"

Lindsey begins to speak, "I think I'd rather look at three elderly people having a threesome on a park bench than witness what I just witnessed again. Please, for the women and children, never do that again. Ever." She speaks for all of us.

"You liked it," he says, winking at Lindsey. "You're up, suga!"

Lindsey walks up and grabs a ball. "Here goes nothing." She rolls the ball down the lane, connecting with the pins and causes eight of them to tumble over.

"Close, but no cigar!" Nick yells. "Not everyone can be as good as me. It's okay, Lindsey."

She doesn't say anything and grabs another ball. I never really thought about it, but she does have a big ass. Like, it's kind of pretty. You know…round. Can butts be pretty? It's the strangest thing in the world that men find butts attractive. Personally, I think it's hilarious. And even though I agree with it, I still find it strange.

She walks up and throws the ball, knocking the other two pins over. She looks back at Nick. "Suck my left titty," she says.

I wonder why her left titty should be sucked and not her right. It doesn't make sense to me.

We finish the ten frames. I come in last, of course, and Nick finishes in front of me. The only female of the group wins by a landslide with a score of 215. I receive a score of 89. Low, but better than the kid in the wheelchair bowling with bumpers beside me.

On the way home, Lindsey decides to not put her smelly, and now infected, feet with the freckle I never noticed before in my face. She sits in the front seat while I'm in the back, listening to the same playlist we listened to on our way to the bowling alley. Siting in the back, no talking, just listening to Tyler Joseph sing about trees.

"I'm telling you, Melon, you'll like it," Jordyn says. She showed up at my house without telling me and decided it would be a good idea to put a blindfold over my face and drag me to this undisclosed place. For all I know, it could be a cult gathering or an all-day cooking class. I realize those are two extremes on the opposite side of the spectra, like democrats and republicans.

"Is the blindfold really necessary?" I ask her. "I mean, what if you look out the window and a huge fucking deer is running in front of us and you're about to hit it and I can't reach over and grab the wheel 'cuz you're looking out the window at a park or a mother and her baby or something."

She looks at me, wearing a face of displeasure. I'm wearing a blindfold, and I know it's a look of displeasure. "Okay, firstly, please don't cuss around me. I'm not a big fan of cussing. I let you off the hook at the bar because you were totally drunk, but no more. Secondly, I will ignore the fact that you just made an extremely sexist comment. I forgive you because of the sure fact that you are blindfolded and probably uncomfortable."

She gets me. And if it takes not cussing to grow closer with her, that's what I'll do. I'm not sure why I cuss in the first place.

"Yes, I apologize, sincerely," I say. I mean it too. "But where are we going?"

She ignores my question. We continue driving for an hour or so. She talks about her life and how she wants to transfer schools this upcoming fall. She tells me that her friends are a bunch of whores, and she doesn't want to finish school with them.

"I'm not a whore though," she reminds me. She wants to know what it's like to have real friends at a school where she "belongs."

I guess at her old school she and her friends were on top of the food chain, hence the whole whore situation. All the girls wanted to be them, and all the boys wanted to do them. Jordyn didn't like who she was. She didn't like how girls looked at her; didn't like how her friends treated other people. The whole thing is shit.

She wants to spend time with people who don't think about hooking up and boys and dick. But most of all, she wants to spend time with people who would drive an hour blindfolded, not knowing where they're going. So hopefully she decides to transfer to my school.

I don't really get tired of listening to her speak. Her voice is quiet and soft. She uses words like, *dope* and *lit* to describe certain things. She explains to me that *lit* means crazy and fun. She talks about her family and her love for Jesus. She hadn't explained to me about her love for Jesus prior to this car ride. She's Catholic and goes to church every Sunday. She has Bible study every Tuesday but doesn't really like it because they mainly play games. She likes games, but no game should interfere with Jesus Christ.

She's just great. Everything about her.

We listen to a variety of music on the way up to the mystery place: Post Malone, Tauren Wells, Jon Pardi. I tried to convince her to play Twenty-One Pilots for a song, and she refused. She wants me to go outside my comfort zone.

I reply with, "I'm blindfolded," and she laughs.

After a quick pit stop at a McDonald's for a piss, Jordyn says we're almost there. Jordyn kindly lets me remove my blindfold for my bathroom break and forces it back on my head when I get back in the car.

Only a few minutes later, she tells me to take off my blindfold for good. "It's only because I don't want you to know how to get here. It's my secret spot that no one knows about." She gets serious when she says these words. Her voice wasn't soft and quiet, but stern and strict. She wants to let me know how serious she was about this.

I take off the long piece of fabric that was covering my eyes, blink a few times due to the blinding light, and begin searching for where I am. Nothing looks familiar. I have never been here. We are driving down this road; no cars accompany us. Nothing surrounds us except forest on both sides. The road is big enough for one car, just one. So if a car is going to come toward us, we're going to have to pull into the forest and wait for it to go by. But my guess is no car is going to come toward us.

We drive another minute or so and Jordyn begins to brake, and we pull over to the side of the abandoned road. I'm expecting Bigfoot to come out and look at us, thinking to himself how these two kids found his secret spot in the middle of butt-fuck nowhere.

She gets out of the car and I quickly do the same. She walks around the car and grabs my hand. Her fingers, soft and cold, wrap themselves around mine, her touch so delicate it couldn't hurt me if it wanted to. She begins to walk into the dark and cold forest. I can't hear a thing except for branches breaking beneath our feet after every step we take.

"Okay," she begins to say, breaking the silence. "When I was an infant, I was a horror for my mom and dad. I'm talking I would cry over everything. Even when I was four or five, this continued, and I kept crying until I got what I wanted."

"Maybe you should keep crying until your parents say you can transfer schools," I say, winking at her.

She tries to hide her laugh, letting me know it's not a time to joke about anything. "Not the time, Melon. I'm trying to get deep with you here, man."

I laugh, and I motion my head to tell her to keep going.

"So, I guess they finally discovered I like car rides. So one day when I was five, we took a drive, and we parked our car exactly where I parked today. We lived in the same house then, so it was about an hour and a half or so. A long time in the car with a five-year-old. But I liked it. I liked the wind in my hair, and I liked listening to the music on the radio.

"I wasn't sure why they stopped at the time, but they did, and they both got out of the car and they took me out of my car seat and we walked the same path we're walking right now to the same place where we're going. And my dad was holding my hand, similar to the way I'm holding yours right now. Which is very sweaty. You should probably get that checked out by the way."

"Not the time to joke, Jordyn," I say, sarcastically. All of a sudden out of the corner of my eye I notice a squirrel. He's not walking, just sitting very still. And far off in the distance I can hear water, very faint. Like water splashing water, not resting water.

She continues, "They didn't say anything to me. Not where we were going or anything. After a couple minutes, I heard water in the distance. And that's what we were walking towards. It was nice and peaceful. I saw different birds and deer and squirrels and a whole bunch of other forms of life." Then she stops talking and the silence comes back again.

To our left, I see a deer. Not necessarily big, but still a deer. It must be a doe then. Its eyes are piercing, fixated on me and nothing else, not moving. We keep walking, and it seems like Jordyn doesn't even notice the deer. Maybe she does, but it doesn't appear so. She would've looked at it or something.

We continue walking toward the sound of the water. It keeps getting louder and louder with each stride we take. I can see a small stream of flowing water about 100 yards away. The birds are singing now, making the silence a little more peaceful.

"It's right up here," she says excitedly. She pulls my arm and now we're jogging. Not running, but more of a soft jog. Enough to make my hand sweat more. That's the best thing about this; she hasn't let go of my hand once.

She begins to talk louder. She must because the sound of the water is becoming louder and louder. "By the end of the walk, I was exhausted, and I was crying because my feet hurt, and I was crying because I wanted to go back in the car and keep driving."

We start slowing down when we reach the small stream of water. I feel it in my shoe. It's cool. Not cold, but cool. I probably should be worried that my favorite pair of shoes have a hole in them, but that's the last thing on my mind.

I look forward, seeing a huge drop-off in a couple of steps. It's amazing. I see nothing but forest for miles. The sound of the water is beautiful. You can hear it falling off the cliff and smacking rocks down beneath. The water flowing down the waterfall is clear and pure, allowing us to see the bottom.

"Welcome to my world, Melon," she says looking back at me. The smile on her face is priceless, a smile from cheek to cheek, dimples showing. Her cheeks are a soft red. She lets go of my hand and walks closer to the waterfall.

"Holy shit," I say. Her eyes zoom onto mine. Knowing why she did that, I say, "I'm sorry. No cussing. But it's, honest to god, the most beautiful thing I've ever seen." Lie. She's the most beautiful thing I've seen.

"Isn't it?" she says, smirking. "My parents brought me here, and I stopped crying and my feet stopped hurting and I just stopped. I looked and I listened. It was the first time I stopped crying in five years besides when I was eating or in the car. Look at it. Listen."

I did what I was told and I looked and I listened. The water, flowing through my shoes making my socks wet, and hitting the water and rocks beneath us. The sound of frogs jumping and crash landing, making a big splash in the water. The sight of miles and miles of nothing but trees and nature are indescribable. The clouds covering the sky, barely making the light blue color visible. The birds are still singing, causing a slight smile to emerge on my face. It's only slight because I'm still taking it all in.

She looks at me. "Wanna jump?" Is she crazy?

"Yeah, sure," I reply. Now I'm the crazy one. She has this way about making these things sound so easy. She always gets me to do what she wants me to do.

I wrestle my shirt off and drop it beside me, close to the water but not in it. I take my shoes and socks off and toss them next to my shirt. She takes her shirt off, showing me her pink sports bra. Her breasts are showing but aren't revealed. I feel something growing in my pants but quickly adjust so it's not noticeable. I don't think she saw me looking.

We both keep our shorts on; hers shorter than mine. Her black-and-pink running shorts match her pink sports bra perfectly. And my white shorts match my pasty white skin perfectly.

"Dang, Melon. You need to work out or something." I laugh because I know it's the truth. I look down and see my rip cage peeking out of my skin. "You also have some sharp nipples."

"I'm fully aware. Thanks for pointing those insecurities out." I don't mean it. I'm just giving her a hard time. She reaches her hand out and I take it.

"Hey, look at you, not sweaty. Proud of you." And she doesn't say another word. I look at her eyes and she stares back at mine. She snaps her neck toward the cliff and jumps, pulling me with her.

While plummeting to the cool water beneath us, a plethora of different thoughts enter my mind. *Why did she take me here? Hey, look a deer! I wonder if my dick will become extremely small when I hit the water. It probably will. This waterfall is really big.* And, *She is the most beautiful girl I have ever seen jump off a cliff.*

The wind blowing my hair back suddenly stops when I hit the water. My body goes under, followed by my head. Water shoots up my nose, causing me to quickly throw my hand up to it, plugging my nostrils before more enters. I open my eyes and see Jordyn underneath the water with me. I feel my arm get tickled by her fingers, which are already pruned. Her hair flowing in the water looks even more beautiful than it does above the surface.

I swim my way up, the sun hitting my face as soon as it exits the water. She rises from the water as well, a few seconds after me. The sun is reflecting off the water and hitting her face, making her cheeks redder and making her eyes sparkle just a little more than usual.

"How do you feel?" she asks me with the same big smile on her face that she had before we jumped.

"Spectacular," I say. "That was *dope*." I wink at her.

Her smile gets bigger, which makes my smile grow. "C'mon. Let's sun dry." We swim over to where the dirt meets the water. A big rock awaits our butts while we sun dry. I get out of the water with Jordyn right behind me and sit on the big rock. She sits down right beside me. The rock could probably fit another two or three people. It's that big.

"Tell me more about this place," I say.

"My mom told me that she and my dad used to come up here when they were in college and take night swims and then fall asleep to the sound of the waterfall. They found it by accident. When I was a kid, my mom had told me they took a class field trip to this place in the third grade, but when I was older she told me how she really found it.

"My parents used to find exotic places to bang each other when they were in college. One day, when they were both sophomores, they had been dating a while and decided to take a drive. They had thoughts about doing it in the car but thought the police would come and catch them."

I stop her. "They thought it would be a good idea to not have sex in the car but to do it in the woods?" Sounds kind of dumb.

"You're telling me, Melon. I told them what a stupid idea that was. They could've been eaten by a bear or attacked by Bigfoot or something like that. But that's who my parents were. They were spontaneous and young and in love. They didn't care what happened to them. As long as they were together, it didn't matter if they were attacked or eaten."

"So that's where you get it?" I ask. "That's where you get your live life to the fullest bullcrap?" I figured *crap* isn't the nicest word, but better than the alternative; definitely not a cuss word.

"It's not bullshit, Melon. I'm serious when I say that shit." Her tone changes and her eyes darken. Her mood is completely different. I place my hand on her shoulder, not even aroused by the fact I was touching her without her shirt on, her pink sports bra the only thing from her breasts popping out.

"Are you okay?" I ask her. I start rubbing her shoulder and her back. She leans in toward me, head hanging low, tears beginning to trickle from her eyes to her cheeks. Her red cheeks begin to dim, getting closer to the color of the rest of her face.

"I haven't told you that my father has died, have I?" Her head remains between her legs.

"No," I say, continuing to rub her back.

"A couple years ago, he died from cancer. I was only thirteen, and I had to see my father die from fucking cancer." She's sobbing at this point. It's crazy how fast someone can go from fine to sobbing. She can still get words out, but the tears flooding down her face make me want to cry as well. I take my other hand and start wiping the tears from her eyes, but she slaps my hand away and retreats, only the littlest bit.

"It was terrible and really fucking tragic. But during his last days, I always remembered this place and thought about him and my mom coming up here and taking night swims and falling asleep to the waterfall. I would think about how young they must've felt and how madly in love they once were. Nothing could stop them and their love for each other. They had their entire lives ahead of them.

"Have you ever thought about how young we are? We're truly in the prime of our existence. We do things that we'll never be able to do again and feel things we won't be able to feel when we get older. We're experiencing things for the first time and we'll be able to remember them for as long as we live. We're so fucking fortunate. Too fortunate for our own good sometimes…"

She then comes full circle and starts on again about her parents. "Then, *boom*, a couple years later, they had me, and then thirteen years later, he's dead. Dead from fucking cancer, and he had to leave his four favorite things behind to be sucked up by this fucked up world."

The pain in her voice is real, I know because she's cussing. The emotion behind her tears is not fabricated. I suddenly begin to cry alongside her, unable to hold back my tears any longer. I keep rubbing her back. I look away from her for the first time since beginning her story, before she told me that her father had died. Before tears started to run down her face. And there we are, sitting in complete silence, crying our eyes out, tears running down our faces just like the small stream of water flowing down the waterfall.

This waterfall is a special place, which means she trusts me. This story has a lot of pain to it, which means she trusts me. So why do I still feel like somethings missing?

She apologizes for telling me about her dad. Then I tell her that she doesn't ever have to apologize for anything when she's around me. She could kick me in the scrotum, and I would apologize for having my sack in front of her foot.

Eventually, Jordyn stops crying. It's always sad to see someone sad. That's why I began to cry because I can't stand to see anyone else in tears, especially her. I've stopped crying for a while now, but I kept rubbing her back. She tells me she must get back home because she has plans with Elliot tonight. I know Elliot is her boyfriend. I didn't ask, but I know.

We walk up the hill right beside the waterfall to retrieve our clothes. Ants are crawling on my shirt and shoes, making a home right before my eyes. I shake them off and put my shirt back on. My feet aren't completely dry, so I decide to walk back to the car, carrying my socks and shoes, competing for dirtiest feet with Lindsey.

The walk back is quiet. The deer and the squirrel I saw on my walk to the waterfall have now disappeared. I remember the anticipation of the walk to the waterfall. Jordyn holding my hand. The feeling of being the only two people on the planet. And I realize something...

Being with her. Kidnapping me. Being fucking blindfolded for over an hour. Taking me to somewhere I had never been before. Showing me her favorite place in the entire world. Hearing the story about her dad and mom. I lived today.

Because of Jordyn.

July 20, 2017

I've decided not to tell anyone about my day with Jordyn. How could I? I can't tell my parents because my dad won't care, and my mom will tell me to bring Jordyn over to the house for dinner. She was convinced Lindsey and I were dating for a year and a half before I forced Lindsey to tell her that she was a lesbian. I told her myself for a year before that, and she didn't believe me. She's a bit obsessive when it comes to girls and relationships. But she just wants the best for me.

I can't tell my friends because they will just tell me I needed to bang her, even though Lindsey is the only one out of the four of us that has actually had sex with another human being. It's a long story, but for Nick's sixteenth birthday party, Drew and I decided to get him a sex doll. And he fucked that thing like it was Kate Upton or something. Not saying Kate Upton is just a body to have sex with, but her body is a 10/10—20/20 on Jordyn's scale.

Instead, I decide to write about it for my summer English assignment. I leave out the personal parts, clearly. I don't want to ruin anything between us. I don't want her to be mad at me for telling someone about her life. It's secret, and I respect that.

I spend the day writing. I don't finish, but I come close. I'll only tell Jordyn about the assignment if she asks. If she wants to read it, she obviously can but if she doesn't, that's fine too.

I receive a surprise text message from Jake around 6:00:

> Hey, man. Want to come over and play COD?

Why does he text me? Shouldn't he be hanging out with Jaret Miller or Ian? I don't understand what he would want to do with me. Play COD, obviously…

I respond:

Sure, man. I'll be over in fifteen minutes

I stop writing and close my notebook. I toss my pencil down and get up, going to the key holder that is on a little table to the right of the door. A complete waste of money is buying a stupid table that has no purpose other than to hold a basket that we call a "key holder." An even bigger waste of money is buying a small basket on top of that shitty little table that we consider a "key holder" that holds three sets of keys: my car keys, dad's car keys, mom's car keys. What about the door key? Our door is unlocked 24-7. We don't need to worry about wasting more money to buy a key to the door.

I grab the Disney lanyard that the keys to the reliable green Saturn hang onto and bust out the door, kind of eager to see Jake for the first time in a while. I walk out the door, manually unlock the driver's seat door because investing in an automatic lock for the car is a "waste of money" and drive off to see Jake.

I text him when I make it to his house, and he opens the front door a couple minutes later. It's kind of a shame that the era of knocking on people's doors is gone. The only people that do are salesmen and the Men of the Bible, the people that go around from door to door reading scriptures to try to spread the word of God.

Jake's house is nice. On the outside, it looks boring—a one-floor house painted yellow looks boring to a blind woman. But the inside is beautiful. A wood floor that has the most amazing furniture resting on it. The family room is carpeted, but it is the only room that is. The sixty-inch TV is hanging from the wall, above the fireplace, surrounded by family pictures on all sides. Jake was a cute kid according to their family pictures. But when a boy is around the age of thirteen, this thing called puberty hits. Puberty was not so kind for Jake. Pimples are still left remaining on his face and the weight he gained from overeating has still not left.

He takes me up to his room where the PS4 is still intact and not broken from his constant temper tantrums after being killed in COD. His room is painted scarlet and grey for the hometown Ohio State Buckeyes. Jake is a big sports fan. I guess him overeating and being fat made him realize that he will never be able to play sports, so he enjoys watching them, especially Ohio State.

We are both silent, both not knowing where to begin. Not knowing what to say and how we should say it. I eventually break the silence by asking him how Jaret Miller and Ian are. I don't really want to know how they are; I just want to start talking to my best friend. I miss him.

"They're good, man," he says, turning on the PS4. They can be turned on by using the controller now. I guess there's a button in the middle of the controller which held long enough, turns on the console. "They're out at the bar right now actually. They love partying man. That's all they do. Fuck and party."

"And have you begun living that lifestyle? You know. Fucking and partying?" I seriously want to know.

"Partying? Yes. Fucking? No. Look at me, man." he says this and gets up. He goes to the mini fridge and grabs a Coke. He looks like he's gained a couple pounds since I've last seen him, which was only ten days ago. "I like drinking Coke, and they like working out. There's a pretty big difference between me and them."

I feel kind of sad for Jake. I pity him, actually. All he wants is to fit in. He wants to be one of the cool, popular kids. He's trying so hard to fit in with these athletes and cool guys, he lost himself in the process and left his real friends out to dry.

"You think, man?" I say. "You're completely different than them, bro. Why are you friends with them in the first place? What did they say to you that night at that party? It made you want to become friends with them?"

He draws his focus to me. His eyes are off the screen which now has some sort of solider on it with the loading sign in the bottom right. He gets serious.

"Truth is, man, it wasn't them that made me want to leave you guys. It was me."

Well, shit. If that isn't the next big quote in the upcoming Nickolas Sparks book, I don't know what is.

In disbelief, I ask, "What do you mean?"

"I mean we've been best friends for a long time. We did the same thing every day for years and years. We would go to school to be noticed by no one. We would come home from school, only to be welcomed by our parents and sofas. We didn't *do* anything."

"So what are you saying?" I ask. And I'm serious when I ask this.

"I'm saying that I wanted a change of scenery."

The game is loaded by now and draws Jake's attention once again. I start making my class, trying to pick the best gun possible. Jake is doing the same, choosing the bazooka as his secondary weapon.

"You wanted to dump us, so you can live life in a better way?"

"Not necessarily better, man. Not at all. I wanted a different lifestyle for the summer. I wanted to see what it would be like to do something that wasn't natural. Not something I grew up doing."

"I've heard a lot of people grow up drinking and going to the bar every other night," I say, half joking and half serious.

"You know what I mean."

Part of me understands. That's exactly what Jordyn is doing right now; looking to transfer schools to get away from her friends. "A fresh start." I never thought Jake would do that to me, though. And Lindsey. And Drew. And Nick. We've all been here for him and he leaves without giving us a reason for the longest amount of time. Then now, while we're playing COD, he decides to tell me the truth.

"I forgive you," I say truthfully. "You could've told us why you're doing this before tonight. But I forgive you."

"Thanks, man," he says. "I'm not necessarily looking for forgiveness, but thanks. I promise by the time this fall rolls around, I'll be back hanging out with you guys. I just wanted to see what it would be like."

"What's *it*?" I ask.

"*Fun.*"

I think it's time for everyone to meet Jordyn. It hasn't even been two weeks since I've known her, but I like her, and I have a feeling everybody else will too. I take my phone out and text Lindsey, Drew, and Nick. I tell them to meet me at the bowling alley in twenty minutes. That should give me enough time to text Jordyn and pick her up.

I text Jordyn next to ask her if she wants to go to the bowling alley and meet all my other friends. It's quite fascinating what technology has allowed us to do. She responds three minutes later:

> Sounds lovely, Melon. You think it's cool if
> Elliot comes and meets us there?

Of course she wants to bring her boyfriend. Who wouldn't want to bring their boyfriend to a crummy bowling alley to meet some of the weirdest people on this entire planet? I don't want him to come.

> Sure, tell him to get there in seventeen min-
> utes. Omw.

How can I say no to her?

I pull into her driveway eight minutes later, giving us nine minutes to get to the bowling alley. Lindsey hates being late to places so if I say twenty minutes, I better be there in nineteen.

She comes running out in a Cleveland Indians baseball jersey and shorts that cannot even be seen due to the length of the jersey. She pulls open the door and flops in the passenger seat.

"Big baseball fan?" I ask her. She looks great in that jersey. I notice she's wearing makeup for the first time too. I just now realized that she hadn't worn makeup for any of the times we've hung out. Not even the first night I met her.

"I don't give a crap about baseball," she says. I pull out of the driveway and start making my way to the bowling alley. A kid in a wheelchair rolls by me on the sidewalk, the same kid that bowled next to me a couple days ago. Only this time he had a little girl on the back of his chair, holding on for her life, yelling at the top of her lungs. A child, probably seven or eight.

"Why are you wearing that thing, then? My brother would love it if you don't want it." Why did I even say that?

"Elliot gave it to me," she says with a smirk on her face.

"Aw, Elliot," I say, trying not to let her hear the disappointment in my voice. Not even disappointment. It's more discouraging than anything.

"Aw," she repeats back. The girl on the back of the wheelchair has gotten off and is now sitting on the boy's lap. I turn the corner and they disappear from my rearview mirror.

Jordyn messes with the radio for a while until falling on a song that I've never heard before. It's a song called "Silly Boy" from the band The Blue Van, according to Jordyn. She then proceeds to tell me all the facts about this band I've never heard of before.

"This band is from Denmark, and they met each other when they were in the sixth grade." Her voice is filled with excitement, even though the words coming out are nothing but random facts that I don't care about. "They've played shows in New York before, and they had some of their songs on some TV shows like *Revenge* and *Shameless*." I've never heard of those shows before. I haven't heard of most shows except for *Criminal Minds*. I should watch more shows.

"How do you know this?" I say when she finally finishes. We've made it to the bowling alley by the time she finishes. I don't mind one bit, though. I can listen to her all day. We made it in seven minutes, too, giving us time to walk in. Which is good because Lindsey's car is in the parking lot.

"I know a lot of useless information. My mom says I get it from my dad, but that doesn't make sense because it's not like a gene that's inherited."

"She's being nice," I tell her.

"I get that. But I don't want to resemble my father in stupid ways like that. I want to resemble my father in ways that matter. Like personality traits and the way he handled situations…not memorizing dumb facts."

We walk in the front door, and we see Lindsey, Drew, and Nick getting their shoes from the same creepy man. His mustache is a little longer now. A little chunk of food is hanging on from the top of the mustache, just like last time, probably feeling depressed that he's living his final moments of his life living in a creepy guy's mustache.

They walk away when we start walking toward the counter. I insisted on buying Jordyn's hour of bowling and her shoes, but she doesn't let me. I am trying to be chivalrous, proving to her that it's still living. She will not allow it.

They turn around after I call Lindsey's name. When we start walking, they don't move. Lindsey's eyes are open wide, like if she had just seen a ghost. Nick's jaw drops to the floor, drool coming out of his mouth, reminding me of the stream flowing off and into the waterfall. Drew takes a step back and shuts his eyes, opening them seconds later with a shocked look on his face. All three of them don't say anything.

"I'm Jordyn," she spits out. She seems nervous. Maybe scared? I don't know which one yet.

The awkward confrontation continues when no one says a word for quite a while. I decide to say something, trying to relieve the tension, or whatever the fuck just happened.

"Guys," I begin. "This is Jordyn Marie Wright. The girl I've told you about."

"Just Jordyn," she adds. "I'm Jordyn," she says again. The scared look hasn't faded away yet. It would be nice if my friends decide to say something sometime soon. Otherwise, Nick may get lockjaw.

"Jordyn!" Lindsey yells, her eyes finally back to normal "Jordyn, Jordyn, Jordyn! We've heard great things about you." Who is she, my mother?

"Same about you," she says back. She's amazing. I haven't said one word about my friends to her.

I introduce everyone. "Jordyn, this is Lindsey, Drew, and Nick. Lindsey, Drew, Nick, this is Jordyn." Nick's jaw finally closes, and Drew walks forward a little more, making it a normal distance to have a conversation. Everyone shakes hands, and me and Jordyn get our shoes. She has small feet, which I never noticed before.

Not the best first impression, but it'll have to do.

Sensory overload commences when we reach our lane, and the knocking of the pins and the screaming of the children finally kicks in. Children are to our right and teenagers are to our left—two pitchers deep, might I add. They're yelling at one another, telling each other to bowl faster and which one of them should fuckJamie Collins tonight.

"Those guys are from my school," Jordyn says, slipping her right shoe on first, followed by her left. She has on pink socks that match her pink sports bra which is probably underneath the Cleveland Indians jersey. "And Jamie Collins is one of my best friends," she adds. She throws the air quotes around Jamie Collins when she says this.

"Was one of your best friends," I whisper into her ear. "You have the fantastic four directly in front of your eyes."

Jordyn looks up and notices Lindsey putting on her shoes. No socks again for her.

"Socks optional?" Jordyn says, laughing.

"I don't like to conform into what society wants me to be. Society wants me to wear socks while I bowl, so I do the opposite."

"I like her," Jordyn says, whispering in my ear now.

We begin bowling, trying to tune out all the extracurricular noise about who should fuck Jamie Collins and who should get the first piece of birthday cake. Jordyn walks up and grabs her ball, which is ten pounds, by the way. I normally bowl with an eight, but I had to bowl with an eleven today because she can't bowl with a heavier ball than me. She just can't.

She walks up with this confidence about her. Like she knows she's going to bowl a strike. And just like that, the ball goes speeding down the lane, and ten pins go tumbling over in a heap. She looks back at us and smiles. "My mom made me take lessons as a kid."

Nick leans in. "Holy shit, dude. 105 percent sure she just gave me a mild orgasm."

"Dude," I say. "Chill."

A couple frames pass, and we're all laughing. I knew she would fit in. I just knew. Drew tells her about the time he had to transfer schools to "find himself," but in reality, he transferred because he couldn't take the bullying anymore. Jordyn tells him the same thing, telling the truth, though. She says the transfer is almost finalized. She's going to open enroll in our school this upcoming fall. She hadn't told me before now, so I'm exhilarated. Words can't describe my excitement.

And suddenly Jordyn looks behind me and sees Elliot, walking in the door. She jumps off the badly beat up automount and runs to him, jumping into his arms when she reaches him. He lifts her off the ground, and they spin a circle. Imagine one of those moments in poorly written cinematic history where the girl and her lover haven't seen each other in a while and they lay eyes on one another for the first time. And they run to one another, wind blowing their hair back, and the girl leaps into his arms, being welcomed by her lover like it's the last time they will see each other.

It's like that. Only he wasn't running, she did the running for the both of them. And their hair wasn't flowing in the wind, because of the lack of wind in the bowling alley. The wind was replaced with humidity. My lower lip, sweating like we're sitting on the front porch of a small house in the middle of Africa. I do not believe this is racist, I'm just assuming that Africa is hot due to the placement of it on the math, below the equator.

They kiss before returning to lane 14 where Lindsey continues to bowl. Nick and Drew were watching the show with me. Disappointment swept across their faces, Nick murmurs out, "Damn." And that's the story of the day. Damn.

"Everyone, Melon, this is Elliot!" She seems so happy to introduce him to us. Like he's hers. Like he's a reward, and I got the participation ribbon.

He's strong, veins popping out of his arms like they're about to burst any second. His jawline is chiseled. His abs peek out of his plain white v neck, like the way my ribs peak out of my skin. This guy is not a boy like me. A *man* is the correct word to describe him. No homo.

"Nice to meet you guys," he says firmly. His voice deep, reminding me of a colonel, talking to his soldiers in battle. Except without all the yelling and cussing.

He walks over and sits next to me. Jordyn jumps on his lap, probably crushing Elliot's sack. He doesn't flinch, and they start talking. Whispering, rather. Lindsey is finished with her turn, and Nick pops up next to bowl. Lindsey sits across from me, a look of sorrow on her face. "I'm sorry," she mouths to me. I nod. I hear them whispering, not making out all the words, but I overhear, "baby," and "mine," and "I love you." The last one hurts the most.

Jordyn doesn't talk much the rest of the time we're bowling. She lets Elliot throw a couple balls for her, gutter-balling most of them. He's even worse than me.

"It's okay, babe," she responds to his gutter balls. Then, he tells us that as many dates as they go on, they've only been bowling twice. And bowling is not one of his specialties. I should've responded I'm not one of the fucking blind mice and I can see how horrible he is at bowling, but I said nothing. I didn't want Jordyn to be mad at me.

We leave soon after we finish. Lindsey takes off her shoes and returns them to the man behind the counter. The smell of them makes him pass out. Literally pass the fuck out. It appeared to be the shoes, but it also could've been a heart attack or something worse. No one rushes over to him when he collapses, making me feel a tad sad.

I'm still sitting on the couch, Jordyn and Elliot sitting beside me. I take my shoes off, and they take their shoes off.

We get up at the same time. Elliot is shorter than I imagined. Jordyn being taller than him is kind of embarrassing. In silence, we walk out of the bowling alley. But not before I call 911, because when I drop my shoes off at the counter, the creepy-looking bowling employer is still laying down on the ground. I don't want to feel like a bad guy with a guilty conscience, so I motion someone over to wait with him. Now, I can sleep well tonight.

Jordyn is holding Elliot's hand, just like the way I was holding hers a couple days ago. "I'll talk to you later, Melon!" she yells while getting in Elliot's car. I enter my Saturn, alone, not like the way I entered the bowling alley. Jordyn's perfume is still lingering, making its way throughout my car. I see them drive by me, their hands placed between one another, his right and her left, fingers interlocked. The smile on her face hasn't faded one bit since seeing him.

I pull away, thinking about her smile. The one goal of my friends liking her accomplished, but I'm still leaving hurt. I call Lindsey while turning left on to the main street. I ask her if I can come over and watch some *Criminal Minds*. She says that's okay, but she's having dinner with her parents soon. I tell her don't bother and I drive home, passing by an ambulance that is probably going to the bowling alley. I hope it's nothing serious, just the stench of rotten feet that made him pass out. Unfortunate, but a funny story the creepy man can tell his creepy wife one day.

M y mom wants to have a family dinner tonight, but I don't really want to. I'm a teenager. I told her I want to hang out with my friends and spend time with them because summer is ending quickly. Yet we're having a family dinner because she wants to. She pulled the "I gave birth to you" card, which is unfair.

My brother and dad are in town for the first time in a while. They've been on the road for baseball tournaments, jumping from city to city. One second, they're in Vegas, then Atlanta, then Houston. I can't keep up. To be honest, I don't want to keep up. I don't care enough to want to keep up. My dad still pays the bills, though, so I love him. I hope that doesn't make me a gold digger. And I love my brother, too, in my own weird way.

My dad starts grilling hot dogs and hamburgers out on the patio around five. Until then, I was working on my paper for English—which I finished! It's totally amazing and can't wait to share it with Jordyn, only if she asks to read it though.

The smell from the grill trickles up the flight of stairs and into my room, making me hungry. I wasn't hungry until that point. I walk downstairs, only to see the dining room table with crockpots, filled with food to the very top. The smell is filling up the kitchen, making sense why it went up the stairs into my room as well. I see my two favorite dishes, buffalo chicken dip and cheesy potatoes. My mom doesn't cook too much during the summer because of my brother and dad being gone so much, but when she does, she cooks the whole fucking fridge. Freezer too.

My dad is still grilling and I walk out to try to help him. I'm not really a "hands-on" type of guy. I don't even know how to turn the grill on. I should go out on the back patio more often. Because my dad makes so much money, he invested a lot of time into the back patio. A stone wall surrounds the four tables, red and blue umbrellas sticking out the middle. A fountain of water shaped like a baby shoots water out of its mouth every couple seconds. Another waste of money, joining the likes of the key holder and the table the key holder sits on.

Dad tries teaching me how to "read" the hamburger patties and the hot dog wieners. He tells me that "grilling hamburgers and hot dogs is like sculpting. After years of practice and doing it a specific way, you'll be able to make masterpieces. The perfect work of art." I slightly understand, but why would you compare meat to sculptures?

I think the last time my dad helped me try something new was when he taught me how to ride my bike. It's my first memory—four and a half years young. My dad didn't put training wheels on me because he thought if I had training wheels on, I would never want to take them off, which is a fair assumption. And "only girls and pussies wear training wheels."

I remember it was the perfect day. Almost as perfect as the day Jordyn and I went to the waterfall. There were white clouds covering the sky and the sun slightly showing behind one of them. Every house had their sprinklers on and a lot of old couples were out walking. The man and woman with the son in the wheelchair were out walking. I don't know why I remember that. It was just that great of a day.

Children were out playing hopscotch and four square in the street. They're now in college, I think. They were too big for me to play with, so my dad wouldn't let me. He put me on a bike and held onto my back, pushing me ever so slightly. I try to keep my balance, but when he removes his hands from my back, I fell over.

I began crying. Crying so loudly that the kids who were playing hopscotch and four square stopped playing and stopped hopping. They were worried. My dad picked me up and held me by the shoulders.

"We don't cry," he said. "Only girls and pussies cry." He whispered this in my ear so none of the other kids could hear. The crying started to slow down and then suddenly stopped after a minute or so.

He tried the same thing. He put his left hand in the middle of my shoulder blades and began pushing. A couple strides later, he let go and I fell over. But I didn't cry this time. I couldn't cry in front of my dad ever again. And to this day, I still haven't.

This continued on for two hours. He kept placing his hands on my back and walking a couple strides. Then he would remove his hand and I would fall over. I couldn't stop falling.

Then my dad talked to me. Not sternly, but kindly, soft and sweet. "You're going to get it. If not today, then soon. In life, you're going to meet new challenges and new obstacles, and you're going to have to persevere." I didn't know what this meant at the time. How could I? I was only four and a half.

The first try after having that talk with me, he put his hand in the middle of my shoulder blades and began pushing me. A couple strides later, he let go, and this time, I didn't fall over. I pedaled, and I kept my balance. My dad ran beside me, pumping his arms in the air yelling, "That's my boy! That's my boy!" It was nice to be his boy. And ever since my little brother was born, it hasn't seemed like I have been.

So it's nice spending time with my dad. It's only been thirteen years. Even if it's only grilling hot dogs and hamburgers, I feel like I'm his boy again. I don't have to like him all the time. He does shit that bugs me. He favors my brother too often, forgetting about me too often. But I love him. He used to tell me the bike story every night before I went to bed, showing me how proud he was to be my dad. I just want that again.

Maybe he's disappointed in me? Dads are supposed to love their children unconditionally. But I feel like sometimes dads want their sons to be like them—be interested in the same things they were interested in and act the same way they acted. All dads want to have a big strong son who stands up for what they believe in and are athletic and *brave*. I'm not like that, and my dad has realized that for quite a while now. He sees something in my brother, though, driving him to spend all his time and attention on him, allowing me to slip through the cracks to eat my watermelon all by myself.

We finish our masterpieces around five thirty, finishing up around the same time as my mom, who made cheesecake for dessert.

I sit down at the table, food still throwing steam in the air. I wait for my mom to do the same and give us the signal to start eating.

She finally sits down after being upstairs for a while. That's another mystery in life. Women tend to go upstairs and not return for quite some time. What do they *do* up there? She looks the same way as she did fifteen minutes ago. I need to look into this. Mom asks which one of us wants to lead the family prayer before we eat, which is odd because we've never prayed before dinner, ever. But I bet Jordyn's family prays before every meal.

No one exactly jumps off their ass cheeks to say family prayer, so I raise my hand. Mom looks pleased to see me volunteer, but truth is if I didn't, no one would, and we don't want to make Mom upset when everyone is home for the night.

I begin, "Dear Lord"—Dear Lord? What am I doing, writing him a letter?—"thank you for allowing us to have everyone under one roof for the night, it's been quite a while. And thank you for everything you do. You allow us to grow and live healthy lives every single day. Thank you for this lovely meal my mother and father made. It looks delicious. And then God's people said…"

"Amen," we all say. I don't know exactly what I just said, but it seems to satisfy my mother so I'm happy. My father and brother seem to nod as well.

Mom tells us we can begin eating, and I waste no time. I start with the buffalo chicken dip and then make my way toward the cheesy potatoes. I fill my plate like I haven't eaten in days. I'll probably add a couple pounds after this meal, which won't hurt because I can afford a couple pounds. I decide to go for the hot dogs and hamburgers last because I want to savor that taste. The other two things are my favorite, but I took part in making the hot dogs and hamburgers, so I want them last.

After eating my first plate, my mom asks us to go around the table to see what we did this past week. We used to do it as kids all the time. She would love hearing about our days at school and what we did at recess and all the bullshit parents love. Not parents, mothers.

"I spent the week playing baseball," my brother says. He's not lying, but it wouldn't hurt him to add a few extra details to spice it up a little. Maybe seeing a movie with dad or something in Vegas. I mean hell, he went to Vegas and all he can say is "I spent the week playing baseball"?

"How'd you play?" my mom asks, trying to seem curious. As kids, she always asked follow up questions. I'm not sure if she wanted to or if that was in the mom handbook, but she always asked questions.

"I didn't exactly get to play. But coach said I'll play next tournament!" His coach should just tell him that he's not going to play so if he does play, he'll be excited. The key to happiness in life is low expectations.

"Good, honey. Good," she smiles, probably faking. She nods at me.

"I've spent a lot of time with my friends at the bowling alley. I've met this new girl named Jordyn who is really awesome and cool." Hopefully that answer is good enough. I don't want to tell her everything that's happened this past week, and I don't hype Jordyn up. I don't want my parents asking if she's a future girlfriend or some shit like that.

"That sounds fun!" my mom yells. Her voice is different talking to me than it was talking to my brother. "Is this Jordyn pretty? Maybe I sense a future girlfriend in the picture?" Damn. She can "sense" a future girlfriend? What is she? A fucking wiccan?

My dad seems to take a liking to this conversation. "Answer your mothers' question," he says sternly.

"She asked two questions."

"Answer the first one, first. Then the second one, second."

"Yeah, she's okay, I guess." Lie. She's perfect. "And no. She has a boyfriend." Truth. She does have a boyfriend.

"Sorry," my mom says. She's disappointed, like she's been waiting her entire life for me to get a girlfriend.

"It's okay."

"Is it?" my dad asks.

"Yeah," I answer. Another lie. Sometimes, children must lie to their parents. It spares both sides a lot of time and a lot of effort. Lies don't hurt people, catching people in lies hurts people.

I stop eating before I get full because I don't want my stomach to hurt me the rest of the night. My brother eats a lot and his motto is, "Don't think; just scarf." And I don't like this because if you keep eating, you might die. And I'm not ready to die just yet.

The hamburgers and hotdogs were really good, mostly because of my father, but partly because of me. They were grilled the perfect amount and flipped the perfect number of times. A masterpiece.

Cheesecake is shortly after dinner. We have time to digest the feast we just had and spare some room in our stomachs for one of the most delicious desserts of all time. The three boys gather around the TV, watching some baseball game my brother cares about while my mom cuts the cake up evenly.

"That's a strike!" my dad yells at the television. He does realize they can't hear him, but he says it anyway. He has a beer in his hand, taking a sip every so often. My mom doesn't let him drink at the dinner table, so he saves his drinking until after dinner, which I respect very much.

Baseball is very boring. So I eat my cheesecake very quickly to try to avoid watching more. We're not allowed to eat anything related to dinner in our rooms. Ever since we were kids, we haven't been allowed to. My mom has always believed family time is very important in a young child's "development." As a result of that, we've been forced to eat every weekday dinner in either our family room or a dining room table for the past seventeen years. It's just sometimes we have the entire family, and sometimes we don't.

Soon after I finish my cheesecake, my body tells me I have to poop. I go running upstairs, slamming the door behind me as I enter the bathroom. As soon as I sit down, I start going, letting go a sigh of relief in the process. It's been a couple days since I've gone so it's time to start including more fiber in my diet.

July 24, 2017

I get awoken from my sleep early by the sound of an incoming phone call. Or I've awoken late by an incoming phone call, depending on if you stay up late or wake up early. I never get calls or even text messages during the night, not even from Lindsey, Drew, or Nick, so this is a rare occasion. It's Jordyn, so I suddenly blink my eyes a couple times and slap my face, trying to wake myself up. I don't want it to seem like I was sleeping at 2:15 a.m. in the summer.

I answer, "Hello," trying not to be too groggy.

"Melon," she whispers. She's crying, or at least has been crying. I can tell.

"Are you okay?" I ask, fully awake now. Why is she crying?

"Not exactly," she says. She is currently crying.

"Want me to come over?"

"I can't make you do that?"

"I want to."

"Are you sure?"

"Yes."

"Okay. Please hurry." And with that, I jump out of bed and throw some shorts on. I like sleeping in my underwear because I tend to get hot while I sleep, and I sweat lot. So wearing no clothes is better than wearing clothes.

I creep down the steps, trying not to wake my parents. The buffalo chicken dip is still looming in the kitchen as I walk by. I slip my crocs on at the front door and take my Disney lanyard out of the key holder.

Turning my keys slowly in the ignition (like that's going to make it quieter), I start the car, hoping not to wake my parents. The car's engine is relatively loud because it's an old car. I wait till I'm out of the driveway to turn on my lights, with my parents' bedroom being directly above the garage. I look back through my rearview mirror while driving away, making sure I don't see two screaming parents yelling for their child to get back in the house. Luckily, I don't, and I drive as fast as I can to see Jordyn.

I make good time to her place. It helps that it's 2:19 in the morning, and no one is out on the roads. I dash through the green lights and speed past the red ones, trying to get there as fast as possible.

Jordyn comes walking out the front door, which is surprising because I haven't even texted her I'm at her house yet. She's wearing a long sweater and no pants, not attempting to hide anything from me. Her shoes are missing and her face has makeup running down her cheeks. She's standing still, looking at me as I get out of my car. She doesn't wave and doesn't talk. Sadness has overtaken her body, making it impossible to be herself. It's scary what sadness can do to a person.

I walk up to her, not going in for a hug but just standing there with her, looking at the sadness on her face. "Are you okay?" I ask. Her eyes hanging low, afraid to look up. She looks like the deer in the forest near the waterfall. The deer was motionless, its eyes staring into nothingness. Jordyn's eyes appear to be staring at the ground, but assume she sees nothing but black.

She doesn't answer. The tears have stopped, not allowing her to cry anymore. She moves for the first time, motioning me to walk inside. She puts her index finger to her lips, telling me to be quiet and to not wake her parents.

We creep down the stairs, Jordyn first, then me. I didn't know her bed was in the basement. Baby pictures cover the wall from the moment we start walking down the steps, which are unusually not creaky. There are pictures of all four Wright children. Jordyn and her twin, Tiffany, cover most, but their little sister, Riley, and little brother, Jeff, are in a few. I can't even tell Jordyn and Tiffany apart in most of the pictures. None of the pictures actually.

We reach the bottom. The basement is huge. A giant red sofa sits directly in the middle of it, facing a TV hanging from the wall. Cabinets are on both sides of the TV holding DVDs and VCR tapes.

A pool table is in the corner, accompanied by a ping pong table. Jordyn walks through a door that is next to the pool table.

I follow Jordyn into what appears to be her bedroom, posters covering the walls all around me. Gigantic posters ranging from the Backstreet Boys to Leonardo DiCaprio to a Lamborghini. A fucking Lamborghini. I never would've guessed Jordyn as a car fan, but I'm not judging. It hangs above the top of her bed, where she puts her head to sleep at night.

Her closet door is open, allowing me to lay eyes on her wardrobe, which is extremely large. There's no organization to her closet, proving to me that rompers can be next to winter jackets if one really chooses to place them together. A variety of different kinds of shoes cover the floor of the walk-in closet, ranging from pink high heels to normal black flip-flops to white Vans.

The light blue watermelon dress she wore the day I met her hangs in the middle of the closet, next to a short-sleeved shirt that says, "chick magnet," and a sundress that appears to go just below her kneecaps if worn correctly. Jordyn, before just now, didn't seem to have any flaws, but one potential flaw could be her organizational skills.

She hasn't spoken since I pulled in. She's obviously hurting because she's usually cheerful and energetic. But her energy is replaced with sadness and misery. She pulls a tissue out of the box that is laying on her dresser and attempts to wipe all of the runny makeup off from her face. She doesn't come close to wiping it all off.

"Jordyn," I say quietly. "Talk to me."

She walks over to the unmade bed, white sheets with pink flowers halfway off, flopping on it, causing her legs to flail in the air. Her shirt goes half way up her torso, revealing her stomach that I try not to look at. I try to resist the urge to look, but I can't help it.

She musters up enough courage to speak. Her words are barely loud enough to be heard, but when I lean in a little, I can ever so slightly hear, "He *fucked* Jamie Collins." I can sense she wants to cry again, but tears are refusing to fall out of her eyes, which are still bloodshot. Clearly, it hurts her to say these words, but I'm glad she can say them to me.

"Come again?" I say, not believing the words that had just softly come out of her mouth. Her dresser has a mirror directly in the center of it, causing me to look at both of our reflections. Jordyn, looking sad, and me, standing next to her bedside, not knowing what to say or unsure if I should even be here at all. Actually, for the first time in my life, I know I can't be anywhere else but here. She's important to me, and she's hurting.

"He's been fucking Jamie Collins for a while now," she whispers. I haven't seen this much pain before. Not physical or mental, but emotional. I've seen emotional pain before, but not like this. So much of it bottled up in someone. I suppose emotional pain has the ability to make a stronger impact on someone. My eyes drift off the mirror and onto Jordyn, the non-reflection version of her. Exhausted and fatigued aren't descriptive enough to describe what she looks like.

"Jordyn," I say, slowly squatting onto the end of her bed, opposite of the Lamborghini poster, which should be the last thing on my mind right now. I rest my hand on her foot, which is cold—freezing, actually. She doesn't move fast, but rather curls, steadily into a ball. I keep resting my hand on her cold foot, just hoping my touch solidifies I'm here for her. "He doesn't deserve you."

"He fucked Jamie Collins."

"Jordyn."

"Have you ever been cheated on?"

"You need a significant other in order to be cheated on." I've never had a girlfriend before.

"Don't date." She's serious when she says this. "It's pointless."

"No, it's not," I say.

She sits up, pulling her feet closer to her chest, hugging her knees. She's resting her back on the wall. A young Leonardo DiCaprio is smiling above her.

"Do you want to know how dating goes?"

I nod. I have a feeling she would've told me without my approval anyway.

She inhales deeply, exhales quickly after and begins: "You see someone you like. Someone you think is physically appealing. You have no fucking clue what that person is like 'inside,' and honestly, you don't care. Your initial instinct is based on what that person looks like. People don't care about how caring and sweet you are initially. If you're not good-looking, you don't stand a chance. So all of the fat-asses and the kids with acne covering their face are shit out of luck. They can save as many dogs at the pound and volunteer as much as they want at fucking Red Cross. It doesn't matter."

I've got no chance to date, apparently.

"You decide to walk over to them and say hi and spark up a conversation, right? Well, Melon. Don't. Don't, because this is when the mind-fucking begins. You walk over. You try not to walk too fast, but at the same time, not to slow. You look around the room, trying to avoid eye contact for as long as possible, trying to seem not too eager.

"You finally reach that person. And they smile at you and introduce themselves. And then you do the same. Again, not trying to seem too eager. You don't want to show your vulnerability, even though you are 100 percent vulnerable. There's not one part of your body that isn't vulnerable."

I'm not quite sure why she is telling me this. She wants to tell me why dating is bad but she hasn't even mentioned dating yet. It's all confusing. But I listen, not saying a word to her. Telling her story appears to get her mind off being sad which has just grown into anger. My eyes flicker around her room while she's telling me this, though, providing me a little more insight on what makes Jordyn Marie Wright, herself.

Covering the dresser are pictures of all the Wright's just a few years younger than they currently are now. I see an adult male, easily filling in the missing pieces myself to realize this is Jordyn's dad. All the pictures on the dresser are ones with her dad in between the frames, reminding Jordyn of everything that could've been. I hope Jordyn has these pictures because she wants to remember the good times, not fantasize about the future he should've been a part of.

She starts up again. "He or she is lying to you. If you tell them your favorite color is blue, they're going to say the same. He asks you a question, 'What's your favorite subject in school?' and you say math, they're going to say math too. People lie. It's in our genes."

It's like I said before, lies don't hurt people, catching people in lies do. And it seems like Jordyn has caught Elliot in a lifetime of lies.

"You agree to go out on a date with this someone. YOU DON'T KNOW WHAT YOU'RE GETTING YOURSELF INTO!" She yells this. I'm afraid her family is going to wake up, and truthfully, I really don't want to see them right now. This isn't the best first impression— talking to their crying daughter/sister who is in her underwear, makeup on her face, telling me about her fucked up relationship. It would be a tough one to forget, but not the greatest.

Old sports trophies rest on the white shelves hanging from the nicely painted grey walls that surround me. I can't make them out, but Tiff plays soccer, so I assume she did too. She hasn't talked much about her childhood to me, keeping some parts of her life a mystery. Which hurts because I want to know everything but learning everything about someone you love takes a little longer than two weeks. I wish it didn't though.

"You go somewhere quiet. A movie or something because you don't want to talk much on the first date. You don't want the person you are interested in to see how crazy you are on your first date. Everybody is crazy, Melon, so don't sit there and think to yourself that you are not crazy. Because you are."

I'm not thinking that.

"You really want to hold their hand. The pure sensation of holding a hot guy's hand is overwhelming. It's like you are showing them off. He's yours and no one else's. It's like a fucking floating sign above your head that is following your every move, telling people to look at me holding hands with this guy." *Girl*, in my case.

"After the movie, they tell you that they really like you and you're dumb enough to fall for it and agree to be their girlfriend." *Boyfriend*, in my case. "And you give each other gifts for your one-month anniversary and give more gifts for your two-month anniversary. You kiss each other and make promises you can't keep. You dress up for the slightest occasions, like going to lunch at the fucking food court in the mall.

"Months later, you decide to introduce them to your family. And your family is smart enough to tell you that something is wrong with this person. Something doesn't 'smell right.' But you're hoping they're wrong and you're hoping that young love will win in the end. And your family will apologize at your wedding and tell you how happy they are that you found the one."

I look at my phone, not because I want to go, I just look at it. It's a teenager's habit, looking at their phone. It's like looking at your watch for old people.

"And then, Melon, there's a hiccup. You catch the person that you are now in love with looking at another girl in the restaurant while you're on yet another date, even though you know everything about that other person—likes, dislikes, what they care about, what they don't care about, what makes them mad and what doesn't—everything. And when you're walking to go to the bathroom, you see him smile at that girl, just like the way he smiled at you for the first time.

"But you brush it off. You feel like you deserve what he does to you. You aren't showing him what kind of girlfriend you can be. You've driven him toward looking at other girls. You're not pretty enough or what not. And then you start wearing makeup to show him what you can look like. You 'maximize your potential.'" I don't wear makeup. But, now I know why Jordyn does. She doesn't feel as pretty when she doesn't.

"He looks at you differently, telling you that you're the most beautiful girl in the world. And it's all because of some fucking stuff on your face. Which is not only offensive, but it hurts being told that the fake you is beautiful and the real you isn't good enough. The real you allows him to look at other girls in restaurants."

She hasn't moved since beginning this detailed explanation of dating. Her arms still wrapped around her legs, holding on for dear life. I'm still sitting at the end of bed, my eyes staring at her through the whole thing. I care for her, and she's hurting. I need to show her that I'm here for her.

"He takes you up to his room one night when his parents aren't home. You're smiling because you know what is about to happen, but you're actually really scared and afraid to show it. You tell him you've done it before, but in reality, you haven't. He takes your clothes off.

And there you are, naked in your boyfriend's room, kissing him passionately. Then, Elliot asks you if you want it, and you nod your head. And he kisses your breasts and throws you on the bed, laying still. The feeling of not knowing what do hits you all at once. So you just lay there, very still, hoping it doesn't hurt."

I get upset when I hear her talk about having sex with Elliot. I knew she must've done it with him, but hearing it hurts. I want to be her first and I want to be her last.

"After he finishes, you think to yourself how he can be finished so quickly."

I laugh at this part, and she stops telling her story and she chuckles too, showing a glimpse of a smile. The smile that has been hidden for the entirety I've been here. The most beautiful smile I've seen. But the smile quickly fades and she gets back to the point.

"You lay there on your boyfriend's bed, feeling useless. Understanding that you are just another body to him. You've given him the only leverage you've had left.

"And you spend the rest of your relationship putting on a fake smile. You talk with your family who turned out to be right, and you introduce him to your new friends. And you ignore your new friends because you're trying to mend the broken relationship."

That's me. I'm part of the new friends.

"But lastly you find out that he fucked and has been fucking Jamie Collins for months. He doesn't tell you, but your ex-classmate decides to tell you, someone who saw them having sex at a party not too long ago. And then you break up with Elliot, finally understanding that *I* deserve better."

I'm still sitting very still. When Jordyn is done talking, she doesn't move either. Leonardo DiCaprio stares down on us. Jordyn's shirt is covering her underwear now, saving me from a moment of embarrassment. Again, this shouldn't be on my mind. I guess it's always just on the back of my mind.

"You stayed with him for so long, but yet, you knew he was fucking with your brain?" I know the answer, but I'm curious. Why would she stay with Elliot for that long? Why was she smiling when she was with him?

"Honestly, I was happy too."

"How is that possible?"

"I don't know," she says. She seems fine at this point. I would like to think I am the reason for this, but I know I'm not though. Time helps heal. Talking about anything for a long enough period of time can get your mind off anything. When I was little, my grandmother passed away—I cried for three days straight. And on the fourth day, I was crying, and my mother came up to me and started talking about the family vacation we were about to take. She talked about the food we were going to eat, the waterpark we were going to, and how high the waves were going to be in the ocean. Two hours later, my grandmother wasn't on my mind.

It's weird how some things can be on your mind so much, but then one day it just fades away. There's no fixed amount of time to help heal, it differs from person to person. One day you're thinking about all the pain, then someday the pain is gone. Because I know one thing, pain doesn't last forever.

"I guess, having someone that introduces you as their girlfriend is nice. The feeling of being someone else's…sort of comforting. This feeling of contentment kinda overshadows all the hurt."

I don't agree with this, not one bit. "You can't put your happiness in nobody's hands but yours," I say. And she sits there, not saying a word. Her top lip hides underneath her bottom, making that face people make after seeing a baby. The face that screams, "Aw!" It's hard to describe.

"You're right," she says, exhaling afterward. "Melon, you're so right."

"I know. Am I ever wrong?"

Jordyn laughs at this. And I start laughing. And in my imagination, Leonardo DiCaprio starts laughing too. He would laugh if he was here, I know that much.

We stop laughing and look at each other. Her eyes, still bloodshot, somehow remain pretty. Her face, makeup smeared on her cheeks, remains beautiful. Her hair is tied up in a bun, looking perfect.

"You're amazing," she says quietly.

"You're amazing," I tell her.

She leans in and throws her arms around me. She squeezes me, making me lose my breath for a quick second.

"You're amazing," I say under my breath.

She squeezes me tighter. I didn't think that was possible. Her hug is warm, and I understand the feeling of comfort she had described me not too long ago. I'm not hers and she isn't mine, but I really hope one day, she can be.

Jordyn's family wakes up early, around seven or eight. Until then, we didn't go to sleep. We stayed up, ranking girls and guys on a scale from 1 to 20. I gave her the five categories we use to rank a girl, and she made up her own five for ranking men: Abs, face, ass, hair, height. I'm not gay, but I agree these five categories make or break a man. She's not allowed to rank Elliot, so she ranks a couple of guys at her old school. I have to take her word on it because I don't know them. I wouldn't have helped anyway because I'm not gay, again.

She helps me rank a couple girls. She's seen girls at my school out partying before. Like Julie Ware, complete bitch but a reasonable 18/20. Katie Marielle gets ranked a 17/20. Jordyn helped a lot on her, upgrading her ass from a 14/20 to an 18/20. "Have you seen it in a romper? Fat."

I love Jordyn. She's not the type of girl to yell at me for ranking girls. She doesn't yell at me saying, "Women are not objects!" and I know they aren't, but for the purpose of the game, we have to act like they are. But Jordyn understands that isn't my complete thought process.

When her family starts rustling around upstairs, Jordyn tells me she wants me to meet them. She doesn't want them to know I stayed the night, so very quickly, she makes sure the coast is clear, and I run up the stairs and out the front door. The same front door I walked into earlier today where I saw Jordyn standing there, very still.

I ring the doorbell after a couple minutes of standing on the front porch, the sun shining down on me, burning my skin. She pretends to be confused about seeing me, like she wasn't sure I was coming over this early in the morning.

"Who is that?" yells a boy's voice. I assume it's her little brother, Jeff.

Jordyn welcomes me in and starts walking me to the kitchen. Before, it was too dark to notice the pictures that welcome you inside their house. A family photo of all six of the Wrights smiling at you with writing that says, "Welcome to the Wrights, a place where we're never wrong," underneath. It takes me a second to realize the poor joke attempt, but once I do, I pretend to laugh.

"Nice joke," I say to Jordyn, entering the kitchen.

"Isn't it great?" she says, being serious. "My dad's idea." Now I know why she thinks it's so great. I bet he was a great guy, but I hope he had a different job rather than stand-up comedy.

I look into the family room, laying eyes on a Jordyn lookalike, a teenage girl on her phone, an adolescent boy, and a mom watching TV.

"Mom," Jordyn says. "This is my friend, Melon."

Before I can spit out my real name, she comes running over into the kitchen and hugs me.

"That's a funny name," she says. Her voice sounds similar to that of Jordyn's but not nearly as pretty. She's old, how can it?

Jordyn talks. "It's a metaphor, Mom. You see, girls love apples and bananas and forget how amazing watermelons are."

Jordyn's mom seems confused. I wouldn't bet my house that she was an English major in college. "You can explain that to me later, honey."

"It means," starts Tiffany, Jordyn's twin sister. She looks like Jordyn, almost exactly, but doesn't look nearly as beautiful. She's a little thinner with cuts on her knees that make her tough, but not too tough. She's wearing the Cleveland Indians jersey Jordyn was wearing the other night at the bowling alley, Elliot's present to her. "That Melon here is a very nice guy who enjoys getting friendzoned by pretty girls."

I'm not quite sure how this specific metaphor can give her the idea that I *enjoy* being friendzoned. It's actually the worst fucking thing in the world. Something I hope no boy experiences in their life. "Thank you for the nice guy comment, but no, I do not enjoy being friendzoned." Jordyn chuckles at this.

"Good," Tiffany says. She is still sitting on the couch. She looked at me when she began talking, but quickly turned her head back around, putting a face to the name. Hopefully, she's heard my name before. I want Jordyn to talk about me to her family. I want her family to have an opinion about me already.

I whisper to Jordyn, "Isn't that your jersey?"

She nods. "Me and Tiff have this thing we do after breakups. We wear the gifts our boyfriends got us. I gave her that jersey last night."

"What?" I say in amazement.

"It's an odd coping mechanism, I'm aware. But seeing each other in the other one's clothes makes us realize these gifts weren't sentimental. They're not special."

"How?"

"I wore that jersey for a long time. Too long. Seeing another girl wear it tells me that another girl *can* wear it. I don't feel special having that jersey anymore. It's hard to explain. It just works for us."

Must be a girl thing because I don't understand one fucking word. Most girls just burn their presents from past boyfriends or throw them away. But not Jordyn and Tiffany.

"Riley, Jeff! Come meet, Melon!"

They get up and drag their feet over to the kitchen. Phone still in Riley's hands and a Slim Jim in Jeff's, the breakfast of champions. They shake my hand, telling me they are "pleased to meet me," like it's a job interview. I wonder if they said that to Elliot, announcing they were pleased to meet him.

After shaking my hand, I say, "How are you guys doing?" *How are you guys doing?* What in the actual fuck did I just say? I really said that. These words truthfully exited my mouth in a verbal way. The best first impression I've ever made. How are you guys doing? What the hell?

They don't answer. They shouldn't answer. The guy they just met that they can probably tell is completely in love with their sister just asked them how they are. They're totally and utterly freaked out. Jordyn grabs my hand and takes me to the family room where Tiffany is still on the couch and Jeff went back to eating his Slim Jim and Riley keeps texting her life away, probably making promises she can't keep and sending nudes to boys. I just judged her very harshly for no reason. I take it back.

We watch *700 Club* on TV, and they talk about Jesus and his awakening and how him rising again was the best thing to ever happen to this planet. That's the summary of every episode. Each episode, though, they talk about a different person in the Bible. This episode, they focused on Isaiah, who according to the host of the show, "is one of the most influential prophets in the Hebrew Bible." He was a poet and turned his poetry into prophecies. Many people think, including the host, that these prophecies turned out to be predictions of Jesus. It's all very confusing.

I half listen, and half don't. Jordyn's mother was cooking during the show, which was lucky because she didn't even have to half not listen. She could fully not listen. After the episode, Tiffany and Jordyn begin talking about it, shouting at one another their opinions of Isaiah and whether or not they agree with Pat. I discover the name after the frequent use of it between Jordyn's and Tiffany's conversation; they use it a lot.

Their mom yells breakfast is ready, and we go over and sit in the dining room. Jordyn's mother brings plates over filled with pancakes and waffles, carb overload. Riley complains about having too many carbs for breakfast will make her bloat, which is very annoying. She says, "Having too many carbs will make me have fat rolls, Mom." And their mom says she doesn't have to eat if she doesn't want to and she can make her own meal if she wanted to. She starts eating right after.

Then Mrs. Wright starts asking her kids on what "Father Pat" had to say on today's episode. I'm not even sure he's a "Father." How would she know that he has children? Jordyn tells her this episode was very good, and Pat had some great reasoning behind why he said Isaiah was one of the most influential prophets.

"What did you think, Melon?" she asks me, a waffle halfway down my throat. I start choking, the sudden urge I tend to get after being asked a question I have no idea how to answer.

Jordyn looks worried that I'm about to die, but after coughing a couple times, my throat is clear of waffle and I begin answering her mother's question. "It was good."

Mrs. Wright laughs, along with every other Wright that is at the dining room table. Jeff is laughing so hard he begins to cry. Real tears.

"I'm glad you liked it," Mrs. Wright says.

"I do have a question, though."

"Yes?"

"How do you know Pat is a father? Do you know he has a wife and kids?"

After I say this, the Wrights start really laughing. Jeff is on the ground. Jordyn spits her half-eaten pancake out of her mouth. Tiffany has to excuse herself. Mrs. Wright is starting to choke she's laughing so hard, and Riley is off her phone, laughing. I've done the impossible. I've made Riley Wright drop her phone and begin laughing.

"No, Melon," Jordyn says after the laughter dies down. It was three minutes at least of laughter. "A father, is another name for a priest or minister. A man who leads church services to put it in terms that you'll understand. I had no idea you were this clueless about church and God."

I really am clueless about all that stuff. I've never been to a real church service. My mother and father have never made me go. I classify myself as Presbyterian but couldn't tell you one thing about what it's like and what I believe in and why being Presbyterian is different from being any other type of religion like Judaism or Catholic.

"I've never been."

Riley jumps off her chair. "Hell! Hell!" she yells pointing at me.

Jordyn chimes in, "Stop that, Ri! Just because Melon hasn't gone to church, doesn't mean he can't start." She has my back. "Besides, if you don't go to church, it doesn't mean you're going to Hell. That's why Jesus relies on us to spread his word and trusts us to do His work." She has my back.

Mrs. Wright tosses her a stern look as well. "Agreed. Well put, Jordy. You better watch yourself, young lady. There's nothing wrong about not going to church. Other people have other beliefs." Riley falls back into the chair and looks very unhappy.

"Oh, I believe in God," I say, making sure she understands I'm not a devil worshiper or something. "I'm Presbyterian."

"Very nice," Mrs. Wright says, a grin appearing on her face.

I make sure to have my napkin on my lap and elbows off the table at all times during breakfast. I tell Mrs. Wright, who told me to call her Joanna, what a lovely home she has and how great Jordyn is. What a lovely girl she's raised. All the stuff moms love to hear. There's no greater compliment to mom's than hearing what great children they have and how skinny they look. I made sure to tell her how skinny she looked.

After my belly was finally full after all the carbs (Riley was still eating), I thank Joanna for everything. Everything meaning breakfast and letting me come over to talk to her crying daughter at 2:30 in the morning. But mainly breakfast because she isn't aware of the second thing.

She tells me I'm always welcome and invites me to dinner tomorrow night, a very kind gesture of her. I then get up and walk to the door, Jordyn in front of me. She escorts me out of the house. Does Elliot realize what a gem he's just lost?

"Thanks, Melon. For everything, truly," she says, hugging me after opening the door.

"Thank you, Jordyn Marie. You deserve so much better than Elliot."

She smiles. "I know that now. Thanks, Melon. You're the sweetest."

Walking away, I realize I should've kissed her. No, I shouldn't have. She just broke up with someone. But she called me the sweetest. She talked to me all night. She was in love with Elliot yesterday. She loves me. Of course she doesn't.

I don't have enough fucking stones in my body to kiss a girl who doesn't kiss me first. Leaning in for a kiss that is unwanted might be on the list of Top 5 Worst things that can happen to a young boy, accompanied by (1) A boner in school after your teacher has you answer a question in front of the class; (2) failing a test after telling your parents you thought it was easy; (3) paying for a date with your debit card (and it gets denied); and (4) getting beat up by a girl (and there's no question that it was a "fair fight." You just get your ass kicked).

My mind races a million miles a minute. I drive home, thinking what I should've done a short five minutes ago. I think about the night I've just spent with Jordyn. Thinking about the story she told me. Thinking about her blue underwear. Thinking about *her*.

After an hour or two of driving (I lose track of time when I drive), I call Nick, knowing he wouldn't be up, but figured I'd try. When he doesn't, Jake is next. Luckily, he answers. I really don't want to call Lindsey. She's lesbian, but I am looking for bro talk. For how amazing Jordyn is, she is still a girl. Girls suck the life out of you if you spend enough time with them, in a non-disrespectful type of way.

"Hello?" he says, sounding like I woke him up. Jake has and will always like his sleep. He can truthfully sleep the day away. He's done it before, swear. I'm glad I called Jake, in dire need of his assistance at the moment. He's great, even though I'm not as "fun" as he needs me to be.

I'm excited to hear his voice. "Sup, bitch! Wake up!" I yell at him. Then I begin just yelling at the top of my lungs, "Аннннн!" not saying any words.

"Chill, chill," he says, quietly. His voice is groggy. I definitely woke him up. "I don't like you calling me that," he says after a couple seconds. "I really don't appreciate it." Ironic, because he calls Lindsey that all the time.

"Sorry, my guy," I say, even though he's called people that every day of his life. Plus, I've never said that before. *My guy?*

"You've never said that before." Ha!

"I just thought to myself I've never said that before and you literally said what you just said, and I am astounded."

"What the hell is wrong with you?" he asks.

"A lot of things. A lot of things. Everybody's crazy, Jacob, a wise woman once told me that. A lot of things are wrong with me but being sad is not one. I'm coming to pick you up. Right now. Be there soon. Love you."

He hangs up the phone. I would hang up the phone, too, if I said I love you to myself. I don't blame him at all. Besides, the conversation was done anyway. I just hope he's ready in ten minutes.

I race to his house, windows down, making waves with my arm. The radio is turned up as loud as it can go, and I sing every song, every single one. I even sing this depressing one called "Pale Blue Eyes." I don't know the words, so I just yell random words that match the beat. A very slow beat. The song is sung by this band called Velvet Underground. I assume if I ask Jordyn about them, she would know random facts.

I arrive at Jake's house and immediately begin honking the horn, trying to wake up the entire neighborhood in the process. It's Monday anyway. People should be smelling the flowers and fully awake at 11:30 a.m. on a Monday.

He comes out, scowling toward the car. Disgust on his face, like he's just seen some random guy fucking his little sister. That would put disgust on anyone's face.

"Good morning, sunshine!" I yell to him while he enters the car. "What a day to be alive!"

"What is your deal?" he asks me. He's in pajama pants and an old, ripped up t-shirt that is two sizes too small, revealing his tits. A "smedium" is what people call it.

I show him a big smile, which creeps him out even more. I show all my teeth, revealing pieces of waffle which are stuck. I've been trying to get them out the whole car ride.

"A lot to tell you, man. A lot to tell. Where do you wanna go?"

"Anywhere," he says. "Just stop by McDonalds first. I'm starving."

He rolls his window down as I begin driving, causing his bed head to worsen. I tell him he needs to stop eating fast food, to which he replies, "You live once. If I want to eat fast food, I'm going to eat fast food." I can't argue with that. I'm trying to change my outlook on life. I'm trying to follow the "You only live once motto" as well, listening to Jordyn.

We stop at the McDonalds drive-through. I haven't told him anything yet because he can't listen well with an empty stomach—it's just how he is. He screams his order at the poor man who has to work at McDonalds in the summer to earn a paycheck. "Can I have two Bacon Egg and Cheese McGriddles with no egg please?"

"I'm sorry. We just stopped serving breakfast," the man informs Jake.

"SON OF A BITCH!" screams Jake, yelling at the top of his lungs.

Damn, I hadn't even realized what time it was. I was at Jordyn's house for a little longer than I thought.

"Fine, whatever. I guess I'll have two Big Macs and a medium Chocolate milkshake."

"I'm sorry. Our milkshake machine isn't working right now," the man says, in the same tone as before.

"DAMN IT! Okay, no drink please. Thanks." Jake tells me to pull up before the man can tell him how much he owes.

Jake's mad. "Why don't they ever have the fucking milkshake machine working? I mean, it's a bloody milkshake machine. How can it always be fucking broken?"

I shake my head in disbelief, agreeing with him. Honest to god, it's always broken. It's hard to believe.

The man who spoke to us earlier asks for the money to pay for the two Big Macs. He's an old guy, probably fifties or sixties. A man who had his whole life ahead of him when he was our age. A man who was in love once, planning for his future. His goals were to get rich and have a beautiful wife like most men. And he ends up talking to complete strangers, demanding money, telling his mostly obese customers their milkshake machine is broken.

I want to feel bad for him, honestly. I tend to feel a sense of compassion with strangers who have terrible lives. Middle-aged McDonalds employees are on the list, accompanied by people who live on the street, strippers, and porn stars. But the thing that these people have in common, it's their fault. Porn stars are in desperate need for sex. People who live on the street are all drug dealers and alcoholics (at least, that it what my mother has told me). Strippers tend to be people who rely on their bodies for their future. They are normally the women with big boobs who don't have a backup plan in life or the boys in high school with giant egos that don't apply for college. And lastly, there are the middle-aged McDonalds employees who live in their parent's basement and don't pay any bills and go on Match.com, putting up fake pictures of themselves, trying to catfish twenty-one-year-old hotties. Maybe I'm wrong, though.

After throwing the ten-dollar bill in his face and mumbling, "Keep the change," we sit patiently in the green Saturn, awaiting the arrival of the two Big Macs. They come quickly. I assume they're pre-made and put in a microwave. Jake reaches over me and takes the bag from the old man. I look at him, the old man. His face wrinkled and his hair grey. The face of a man who has had his dreams demoralized. A man who saw his future bright and warm quickly turn into dark and terrible right before his eyes.

I begin to tell Jake everything that happened earlier in the morning as he stuffs his face with a 10,000-calorie Big Mac that will cut his life expectancy by a year or two. He's always been a mighty fine listener when he gets food in his stomach. I'm not sure if he fakes it for my sake, or he really cares that much. But every once in a while, he adds a gasp or a "What the hell?" Plus, he is always nodding and agrees with everything I say.

I finish my story, beginning with the phone call and ending with the drive to his house. Jake is quiet through the whole thing, mainly from shoving food down his whole. "What a night," he says. "Where's your brain at?"

Good question. "I'm not sure. She doesn't like me. There's no way she does. She just broke up with Elliot, who she loved. They were dating for a long time."

He nods. "This is true. But, my friend, she calls your phone at two fifteen in the morning asking you to come over and comfort her. She told you her life lesson that all girls want in life is the feeling of being comforted. and you accomplished that. You made her stop crying and you made her feel better."

I don't like that word *accomplish* in this context. I didn't accomplish anything, I was just there for her, like any nice guy would do.

I didn't think about any of that. I suppose I comforted her and made her feel better, but anyone can do that. That's what it seems anyway. Any boy can pretend to care for someone for so long. I wasn't pretending, obviously, but I need to show her that I can be that guy who comforts her *every* night she's upset.

"How can I prove to her I can be her boyfriend?" I need to show her that I care for her like *that.* Although, I don't want to freak her out and seem like a fucking stalker. There's a good middle ground in between friends and stalkers. And I need that.

"How am I supposed to know?" Valid question. "I haven't had a girlfriend in seventeen and a half years." He thinks for a second. "I actually had a girl that was into me in my preschool class. She kissed me at our Christmas party. I gave her a mechanical pencil when everyone else had No. 2 pencils."

I, honest to god, stop the car. I pull over on the side of the road and stop the car. "Are you kidding me?"

He laughs. "Nope! She caught feelings way too fast."

And I begin laughing. Stopping the car wasn't necessary, but it was for dramatic effect. I had to get my point across on how dumb his little childhood crush was.

We've been driving for an hour or two. Just driving. He kept providing me ideas, none of them worth the risk or worthwhile. Listening to good music and bad. Listening to our favorite people on the radio, Dave and Jimmy talk about nothing. Being on the radio would be a cool job; you get paid to express your opinion.

I drop Jake off around 2:00 because his mom wants him to be home to take care of his sister while she's away at a dentist appointment. Jake's sister is cute. I feel bad for him, though, sometimes. He can't hang out with us occasionally because his mom has him take care of her. She's only three. I understand she needs a break from her occasionally, but one time she had him take care of her because she needed a nap. I thought he was lying when he first told us this.

Jake told me one day she was an accident. And I didn't really need to know that, but it made me think. Adults that age still have sex. Some adults that age don't, but most do. Their sexual desires must be met by their companion. And it's weird for me to think that adults that age do have sex just like young adults do. We're grown to think adults are our superiors and they teach us about Sex Ed and they tell us not to do that shit. But, they do it themselves, even at an old age. I hope I can have sex when I'm that age. And my wiener still works and can get hard when I need it to.

I tell him thanks for listening, and he responds with, "Don't screw it up." I don't know what I would screw up, but I thank him again and drive away. I remember I forgot to text my mom where I was this morning, so I head home afterward. I arrive to my house in disappointment because I was expecting a driveway filled with cop cars. I assumed my mother would've called the police station, filling out a missing child report. I guess she doesn't love me as much as I thought she did.

July 28, 2017

The past couple of days have been incredible. Jordyn and I have been spending a lot of time with one another. Drew, Nick and Lindsey have been good, spending most days at the bowling alley. Lindsey apologized to the creepy shoe guy for making him pass out and he said not to worry about it and told Lindsey she was very pretty. Lindsey then said, "I don't play for your team," and walked out. It was harsh, but she didn't want to get his hopes up, which I understand completely.

Since the drive with Jake, I haven't heard from him. I want to keep him in the loop, but he's too preoccupied with his new friends for the summer. I'm no longer mad at him, just a tad bitter.

Jordyn has been trying to convince me to go to a church service this coming Sunday. I don't want to embarrass myself. I don't know what to expect either. I've been telling her I'd think about it, but I am going to go. I want her to keep asking because this way, I know she really wants me to go. She wouldn't continue to ask if she didn't want me to go.

When I went over for dinner the other night, I sat next to Jordyn and our legs were touching through the whole meal. It was magnificent. She was telling more about her "evolving trust in God." I guess now that Elliot broke up with her, she doesn't want to worry about boys in her life. She doesn't want a boyfriend for a couple months because she wants to "begin loving herself." That's a quote from her.

I really respect Jordyn for this. If you can't love yourself, how do you expect to love someone else? I love this about her. I just wish she would've got dumped a year ago and had all this loving herself shit over with by the time I met her. It would've made this whole situation a lot clearer.

Lindsey texts me, changing our plans from the bowling alley to her house. I didn't want to go to the bowling alley anyway. Listening to the screaming children wears on you after a while. It's like slowly having your ears ripped off your head.

I suspect we are going to watch *Criminal Minds* and order pizzas, which sounds like a lovely night. I ask Lindsey if it's okay if I bring Jordyn and she says, "Just the Fantastic Four tonight, please." I don't mind, no harm in asking. I've been spending a lot of time with her and not a lot with them, so I understand.

I spend my time sitting in my room. I close my eyes, only falling asleep for a couple minutes. Time moves slowly while doing nothing. I'm not sure why this is. I suspect it has something to do with your brain. While doing nothing, your brain isn't fully engaging with activities or some shit, and it makes time feel like it's moving slower than a fucking senior citizen after hearing it's time for their medication. When you're participating in something, like a game or writing something, you are engaging your brain, which makes time move faster. This makes you not think about the time whatsoever and think about the activity at hand. I don't know why I'm thinking about this.

After hours and hours of overthinking about time and who invented the idea of time and how the day was put into twenty-four hours, Lindsey finally texts me, telling me it's okay to come over. Truly, today has been the longest day of my life.

When I arrive at Lindsey's, I spring in the front door without knocking. I figure that I know them well enough by now to not knock every time I arrive. If they know I'm about to come over and they know I'm not a rapist or anything along those lines, why bother knocking?

After making small talk with Lindsey's parents and saying how nice it is to see them, I walk downstairs and see that Drew and Nick are already here. The three of them are sitting on the couch, feet up, enjoying some *Criminal Minds*. I notice JJ on the screen and speed walk over to the couch, positioning myself directly in front of the TV, the best spot to watch JJ.

"Sup, guys," I say to them. "How's JJ looking this episode?"

The three of them turn their heads in unison and look at me like I've just said something idiotic. "Fucking fantastic," Lindsey says. "It's like each curve she has is something special. Like God chose her to be this beautiful for a reason."

"Let me guess. That reason is for you to bang her?" Drew asks.

She nods. "Of course. I would do all the right things to that woman."

The pizza arrives a short while later, and we inhale it down in a matter of minutes, making our stomachs hurt and our shit stink. We finish a couple episodes of *Criminal Minds* after eating our pizza, making that four episodes complete from start to finish since I've arrived.

Lindsey decides that four episodes are enough and quickly begins to provide me ideas on what to do with Jordyn. Not necessarily *do* with Jordyn but gives me ideas on how I should deal with my overwhelming love for her.

"You have a couple options," Lindsey says, holding up three fingers. "One, you could put yourself out there. Tell her how you feel and if you're lucky, she'll feel the same way. Only if you're lucky. It's rare to have someone feel the same way about you."

And I start thinking about how true that is. If people believe in soulmates, and there are seven billion people in the world, I have a one in seven billion chance of finding my soulmate. Which means there is a one in seven billion chance Jordyn is my soulmate.

Even if people don't believe in that sappy shit, finding someone who enjoys your company who also finds you physically appealing is rare on its own. You must overwhelm the person who you are in love with by making her laugh and showing her a good time, while also making him/her horny and wanting you physically. Very tough.

"Option two," Lindsey says, now holding up two fingers. "You can never tell her how you feel, hiding your real feelings for her, either saving yourself from tears, or never finding out that she likes you back and a future with the girl of your dreams."

Relatively scary feeling, knowing that she might enjoy my company the same way I enjoy hers. And I may never find out if I choose option number two. I also save myself from humiliation if she doesn't feel the same way.

Lindsey wiggles three fingers. "Finally, option *tres*. You lie to her. You put her in the friendzone before she can put you into it. By doing this, you can see how she takes it. She would either be fine with it, knowing that there wasn't a future for you two. She could have never liked you and you saved yourself from humiliation by telling her how you truly felt. Or she would be disappointed, telling you how in love with you she really is. Then, you express your love and affection and make fucking love to her."

The third option seems dumb. Lying to Jordyn would mean I have to lie to Jordyn, and I don't think I can convince myself that lying to her is a good idea. Yes, she could be disappointed after I tell her I just want to be friends and watch Nickolas Sparks films with her for the rest of my life. But what purpose does that serve? Then I would just be playing with her emotions. Plus, how would I go about friendzoning her? Do I just walk up to her and say, "I have zero physical attraction towards you and I see no future?" Sounds like bullshit...

"A lot to think about," I say. To be honest, there isn't a lot to think about. I've made up my mind while she was talking. I'm going to drop compliment after compliment to her until she learns that I *like* her. Girls love to be told they look beautiful and they're having a good hair day and stuff like that. If I continue dropping compliments, she will have no other option than to love me. It's physics, really.

We spend the rest of the night talking about senior year and how senior pictures will be arriving soon and where we are going to have lunch every day. We're going to be seniors, so we can leave school during our lunch period. Which is nice because I don't want to spend the only free time I have looking at freshmen eating peanut butter and jelly sandwiches and pineapple cups. This was my meal for the whole year when I was a freshman.

Realizing I'm becoming a senior is terrifying; bittersweet actually. Knowing I'm finished with school and done seeing Jaret Miller and Ian is nice. But life after high school scares me. I don't know what I want to do. I haven't applied to schools. I haven't even thought about applying to schools. I don't know what I want to major in. I don't really know anything. Luckily, there is a community college close to here so there's an alternative plan if it comes down to it.

High school being over means no more high school friends. Well, clearly in this day and age, we can FaceTime and text each other, but that stuff is kinda annoying. It's so much effort to keep in contact with someone when you live far away from them. I'd much rather drive and eat pizza in their basement.

Jordyn, of course, is excluded in this because I see myself with her. So four best friends with Jordyn included, and five best friends including Jake too. I've spent my entire childhood growing up with these people, excluding Jordyn again. Ending high school is just the beginning step of becoming an adult. First high school, then college, and then you find a girlfriend and get her pregnant and start a family. Then, life is finished because you have nothing else to do with your life other than provide for your family and take care of them.

Today, though, I'm happy. I'm not dreading college or hating my job. I'm enjoying my time being young, experiencing things for the first time. It's taken me a long time to figure this out, life being a safe place to live. I want the best every day, proving to myself I'm not a loser. Even though I'm a Melon, I can do things and grow. What Jordyn told me about her father, it's motivating. It's special. And like Jordyn has been preaching, I want to be someone who lives.

Church is weird, especially Jordyn's. As soon as we walk in, we walk into this thing called a "pew." Jordyn reaches down underneath the pew in front of us and grabs this "knee stool." I don't know what else to classify it as so I'm going to call it a knee stool. She pulls it out and then sets her knees on it and bows her head, resting her head on the back of the pew in front of us. This is how Catholics pray apparently.

There is also a lot of singing. A very nice choir that is filled with many elderly people and only one teenager sings us lots of songs, many of them which I don't understand. I understand one and it's called, "Jesus, Thank You." It's easy to figure out what the song is about due to the uncomplicated name. That's why I like it so much.

During the middle of the service, Jordyn explains to me what "communion" is. This is where the people inside the church take turns walking up and eating a piece of bread and drinking "wine" from a glass. The same glass might I add, which is very gross, even though the minister has a cloth to wipe it off in between drinks. They don't use real wine because many children partake in communion too.

Supposedly, the bread is meant to symbolize the body of Christ and the wine is meant to symbolize the blood of Christ. Jordyn adds a bunch of other details that I don't quite understand.

When it's our pew's turn to walk up and retrieve the bread and "wine," I quietly walk up, hanging my head down low directly behind Jordyn. We make our way toward the head minister, whose wrinkles are much more noticeable close up, and grab my bread and sip my "wine." There's a plethora of bread to choose from but I choose white because that's the bread my mom buys for our house. We walk back to our pew, holding my head down the same way I had it walking up.

While the minister is talking during his "sermon," I look around at the church and its beauty. Stained glass paints the windows and golden chandeliers hang down from the ceilings. Pictures of famous people from the Bible are everywhere to be seen. Some clothed and some not. Jordyn points out Adam and Eve to me, and Adam is naked, and his penis is very small. I have nothing to compare it to except for mine. I'm not sure if it makes mine big, or his is just that small. Either way, it should be bigger because Eve is also naked and standing right next to him.

After the service, Jordyn takes me to go get coffee. I guess it's a ritual of hers. After each church service, she goes and gets a regular black coffee at this place called Coffee Expressions. It's very small, but Jordyn calls it cute and petite. I'm not quite sure what is cute and petite about a small coffee shop, but I agree with her anyway. We sit inside the coffee shop, talking about my birthday, which is coming up soon. She tells me she has a big surprise for me and I tell her to not give me a gift.

"Of course, I'm getting my best friend a gift," is what she says back to me. I think to myself that she called me her best friend and best friend is different than boyfriend. Maybe she says this because she doesn't want me to know how she truly feels. But I spend the rest of the time while we're at Coffee Expressions overthinking and over-analyzing the situation. Whether she touched my leg on purpose or on accident. If she bats her eyelashes at every guy she takes to church or I'm lucky enough she only bats them at me.

When we're done, we walk outside, entering the heat. I've dressed up for the church in a suit and tie. I didn't know what to wear and Jordyn told me I looked "dashing." I told her I thought she looked dope, and she really started to laugh. She has this way of making her outfits seem pointless. It's funny how she does it. Most women rely on clothes to make them look beautiful. Jordyn's clothes don't prove her beauty but add to it.

I drive back to her house to drop her off, and she tells me she will see me tomorrow. She thanks me for the coffee and tells me to never pay for her again and waves goodbye to me, standing in the driveway. She never walks inside before I pull away.

I don't let myself drive directly home. I drive around town. There's this place in our city called Old Worthington that I used to go to a lot and sit on a bench and feed the birds and talk to elderly men and women. I decide to do that, so I park my car and walk to my bench, showing my suit and tie to everyone that walks by me. It's my father's, but I like thinking it's mine for a day. It allows me to be somebody else for a while; someone who wears suits and their job in life is to look good. I wish I can have that job.

My bench is empty, but soon won't be. Old Worthington is like Times Square for old people in my city. I assume they are currently eating lunch for their after-church traditions. They will come soon, flooding the sidewalks and causing traffic jams as old people normally do. Meanwhile, I spend my time watching two little kids. Not in a creepy way, though.

They're running in front of their parents, laughing and having a good time. And I begin thinking these kids have their whole lives ahead of them. Currently, they are learning the alphabet and numbers, but before knowing what hit them, will learn about how to write a check and how to drive a car. Fighting with their parents, yelling at them they hate them. But quickly realizing they don't hate them and that they're the best parents they could've asked for. Parents who actually care and allow them to run in front of them in Old Worthington.

Senior citizens come rolling in now. A man named Bill sits next to me and starts asking questions. The typical questions from an old man: your name, age, current school, future plans, etc. The elderly love talking to children and teenagers. They love learning what the new trend is and the new phenomena. They love finding out what kids do for fun and telling them how low gas prices were back when they were kids. Seeing senior citizens smile is so rewarding. We understand they do not have much time left to live, so we need to treat them kindly and make the time they have left delightful.

I talk to Bill until I decide to go home. He tells me it was very nice talking to me and what a great young man I am. He even tells me how nice my suit is! I tell him it was nice meeting him too and walk back to my car and drive home. Even though church was boring, and I didn't understand what they were talking about, spending the morning with Jordyn was nice. It seemed fitting and natural.

Since Jordyn has come into my life, I have this odd feeling. I've always enjoyed my alone time. To this day, I enjoy it. Being alone isn't scary. People always fear isolation and loneliness. Nothing is wrong with it. I've always had my friends to lean back on when I didn't want to be alone, but they won't be around forever.

So now, with Jordyn here, for the first time I can see why people fear loneliness. After you have made a connection with someone, it's a lot harder to be on your own. You have more thoughts and you have more feelings. So much shit is in your head that can make a man go insane.

I suppose there is a downside of opening yourself up.

Walking around the mall is very funny and very satisfying. Not satisfying like an orgasm but satisfying in a different sense. Middle schoolers roam, walking around in high-top shoes with their socks pulled up to their knees and their string bags wrapped around their shoulders. Their hair is slicked back, texting on their iPhones just as much as Riley does.

The girls travel in packs like wild hyenas scavenging for food. All ages of girls walk around the mall, remaining in their packs, though. The middle-school-aged ones tend to wear Uggs, no matter how hot is. Jean shorts are worn tightly around their legs, going down to just above the knees. When I overhear their conversations, it sounds like, "Oh my god! He does not like me! I've tried flirting with him for a month now!" Something along those lines. Flirting in middle school is asking to borrow someone's pencil or texting them, "Hey."

High school girls' packs are different. They like to wear flip-flops, revealing their nicely painted toes. They tend to have on tank tops, showing their shoulders and bra strap. This is the flirting they do. It drives boys crazy. They see the bra, knowing they must walk over and ask for their numbers, but too intimidated to do so because GIRLS TRAVEL IN PACKS. They force men to make a move, showing their passion for them in front of their friends. It's tragic honestly. No man can take that kind of abuse.

Finally, there are college girls. They like to vary their clothing of choice, and sometimes, do not travel in packs, which is rare for the female gender. They aren't there to look pretty but there to shop, rather; looking for new, slutty clothes to try and impress some fraternity brother that only cares about having sex and taking advantage of girls who choose to wear slutty clothes out to parties.

Drew, Nick, and I go inside a shop called Sports Fanatics, which is ironic because we don't like sports. We desperately needed a change of scenery. I love Jordyn and Lindsey, but three boys can only take so much feminine talk.

"What brand of pads to you use?" "Do you like this top on me?" "Eighty dollars for *that* bag?" For the love of God. Clearly, they don't talk about this stuff all the time; I just don't want to hear it at all. If I can avoid this type of talk, I'll live a happy man.

Nick picks up a jersey, yellow as the sun and says CAVS across the front in red writing. "This is the Cleveland Cavaliers! I know it from 2K!" he yells out proudly. You would think he just won the lottery.

He might as well have spoken French to me because I didn't understand a word, except for 2K. That's a game Drew and Nick like to play, but I don't know who the Cleveland Cavaliers are. I can't believe I'm even in a sports store. It's all very overwhelming in my opinion. Jerseys from every team you can think of cover the four walls, even behind the cash register. The only people who are in the store with us are four teenagers wearing jerseys already. Why do you need another jersey when you're currently wearing a jersey? Sports just aren't for me.

I walk my ass outside Sports Fanatics and sit on this giant square sofa that has white tulips on the fabric. I'm disappointed in myself for knowing what white tulips look like. Maybe I've been spending too much time with Jordyn, but probably not. White tulips are her favorite type of flower.

Nick and Drew come crawling out shortly after. "That place is insane!" yells Drew. "See that jersey? Up there? It says Goldberg." He points his index finger at this green jersey with yellow lettering in all caps, GOLDBERG. It's hanging from the very top row in the very corner of the store. I can barely see it from the surprisingly comfy sofa that I'm sitting on.

"Yeah, I see it. What about it?" It doesn't look familiar whatsoever.

"Goldberg isn't even a real person. He's from a movie called *The Mighty Ducks*. I watched it with sister a couple weeks ago. He's some fat-ass goalie. The stereotypical comedic relief in a film, ya know? He was awesome!" He's so excited he actually knows a jersey in a sports store that he doesn't even realize he's showering us with his saliva, causing me to clean my eyes out with my shirt.

Nick overexaggerates. "Jesus Christ, Drew. Why don't you just pour water on us? It'll be quicker." He is one sarcastic son of a bitch. Literally. His mother is 100 percent bitch. I never liked the woman.

"Watch yourself, Nick," I say. "Don't use the Lord's name in vain."

"Don't use the Lord's name in vain?" He busts out laughing, followed by Drew. They even flop on the sofa, kicking their legs in the air, all eyes in the mall on them.

After they're done causing a scene, they stop laughing. "Don't use the Lord's name in Vain?" he repeats again. "What are you saying? Are you, a, I don't know, faggot?"

"Dude, chill," I say. He really uses that word openly. Like, in a mall? That shouldn't be someone's type of humor. No one should use that word. "Don't say that. And I'm trying to learn more about Jesus and respect him more. Oh, and pray more."

"*Respect* him more?"

"Yes," I say exhaling louder. "I want to become a better man and change myself." They look at one another and have the same face, a tiny smirk appearing on each of their faces. They both nod.

"Jordyn," they say to each other, laughing afterward.

We walk to a bookstore called Barnes & Noble. I like to appreciate bookstores because you don't get to see them very often anymore. Society is turning books into audio books. If it's not an audio book, it's a movie about the book. But no one read the book in the first place except for the people in the movie and the people who made the movie. It truly is unfortunate.

We enter Barnes & Noble because I want to surprise Jordyn with a book she really loves. It's called *Night Road*, and she told me a couple days ago. She read it in middle school and really loved it. She claims it's her second favorite book, behind *Abundance of Katherines*. The only reasons she doesn't have it is because Tiffany stole it from her and lost it at a soccer tournament.

I ride the escalator up to the second floor and find it—the last copy, might I add. I take the escalator down and then ride it back up and ride it back down because I love escalators so much. When I was a kid, my mom loved going to Barnes & Noble and instead of searching for books, I rode the escalator. I would ride it up and down, up and down until my mom forced me to stop. She had to promise me a pretzel from Auntie Ann's, which makes the best pretzels. Only a couple times my mother promised and didn't get me a pretzel. After wising up, I would make her pinky swear she would buy me one. And everyone knows you cannot break a pinky promise.

I buy the book and walk out of the store. When Drew and Nick ask me who the book is for, I lie. I tell them it's for my mother. They made fun of me for the Jesus Christ ordeal. Why would I openly give them another opportunity for them to mock me? They know how much I care for her, but yet continue to make fun of me for it. I wonder if they've ever felt love before and that's the reason why they make fun of me; because they're jealous.

Finally, we meet up with Lindsey and Jordyn again. We looked everywhere before finding them, including a store called Coach, which doesn't have to do anything with sports. It's a bag store that sells very expensive and very pretty bags. Neither Jordyn nor Lindsey can afford purses in Coach; not many women can. Their only customers are women who are extremely rich, or women who are currently experiencing a midlife crisis and want to act richer than they really are. This tends to happen to not only women, but men too. I really hope I don't experience a midlife crisis.

Lindsey tells us that they met a really cute girl inside one of the stores they were in, and she got the "lesbian vibe" from her. I'm not quite sure how one senses another girl is lesbian. But Lindsey is very good at this. One time, this girl she really liked was dating a guy. Lindsey told us that she caught a "lesbian whiff" off her. I wasn't aware that lesbians smell different than heterosexual girls, but I guess they do. A couple months later the girl broke up with her boyfriend and came out as gay.

"Hey, Lindsey," I say. "Is a girl 'a lesbian'? Or is a girl 'lesbian'?" I've been wanting to ask this question for a while now, but I never have. I tend to say both, so I want to know which one I should say all the time.

She smiles. "Both are fine." That doesn't help. "I'm going out with her tomorrow night."

Everyone congratulates her, telling her they're so happy for her and how amazing it is she finally met someone. Lindsey deserves a good girl. She tells us all thank you and hopes she can get some "putang" by the end of the night, which is another name for pussy. Most boys will be aroused by this, but not me. The thought of two girls making love with each other isn't sexy. I think about it just like a boy and a girl making love. Love is love, and you shouldn't get aroused.

Walking out of the mall, in desperate need of a hiding place to take a nap, Lindsey suggests going bowling. I really don't want to, but everyone agrees and a minute later, I'm driving Jordyn to the bowling alley.

"Your car sure is crappy," she says. She rubs her hand alongside the interior of the car, feeling every tear and rip. The ceiling hangs low, almost touching the tops of our heads. When it rains, the window tends to leak, dripping little rain drops onto my leg. It's not frustrating, just annoying.

"Oh, is it now?" I ask. "You're more than welcome to walk to the bowling alley if you want." I toss a wink at her.

She laughs. "I'm kidding!" she yells out. Clearly, she's not kidding. It's a horrible car.

"It gets me where I want to go," I tell her. "And that's a sole purpose of a car."

"I love your car," she adds. "It's a watermelon car."

August 3, 2017

Today is my birthday! After living this life without the opportunity to buy cigarettes, lottery tickets or tattoos for seventeen years, I'm finally free to do so by myself! My eighteenth birthday is the second to last meaningful birthday for someone. Everyone loves turning ten because they're two whole hands. Turning thirteen is nice because you're finally a teenager. You can blame your hormones for all the wrong you do. Seventeen is okay because being allowed to see R-rated movies without an adult is the first taste of freedom in a teenager's life. Eighteen, you can vote and do all this reckless shit by yourself. And finally, turning twenty-one is special because people can finally drink with their parents without being ridiculed.

I've been looking forward to this day for a while now. Lindsey, Nick, Drew and Jordyn tell me they have something planned for later tonight, which I'm very excited for. But, until then I'm spending the day with my family. I love my family. But for a child, do we really want to spend the entire day with our family on our eighteenth birthday? I'm guessing most people are on my side, but I'm not going to complain too much though. My dad and my brother skipped their baseball game in Virginia to spend the day with me. So it's nice to feel wanted.

We begin by going to a breakfast place called First Watch. They make the best pancakes on this side of the Mississippi. At least, that's what the sign in front of their store says. They are also all-you-can-eat, which my brother thanks me for. The "don't think, just scarf," mentality is in full effect while we're here. My parents and I are done with our food for forty-five minutes until he finally waves the white flag and throws his fork on his plate. It's a solid effort he made, attempting to beat his record for seven plates of pancakes, three on each plate, he made on New Year's Eve last year. He gets close, eating five plates and two pancakes on the sixth plate. But close only counts in hand grenades and horseshoes.

Next destination is the movie theatre, where we saw *Baby Driver*. I don't tell my parents I've already seen it because I don't want to hurt their feelings. Plus, it was a fucking good movie, and I want to see Ansel kick some ass again. He is truly superb in the movie. I sit next to my brother and my parents sit next to each other. They raise the arm that is blocking them from snuggling, and my mom lays under his arm, placing her hand on my dad's chest. Seeing them cuddle is nice yet repulsive, simultaneously.

I start thinking about how I was conceived, a child's worst nightmare. I can't help myself to not think about it. Did it start by snuggling in the movie theatre? Then I realize that they were about my age when they first met. They fell in love, just like all parents do. I hope all parents were in love at one point. I'm hoping my parents had a spot where they hid from their parents and did teenager shit, similar to the way Jordyn's parents went to the waterfall. I want my parents to have a place like that.

And I want to my parents to keep cuddling and maintain a good relationship. Children don't normally think about these things, but sometimes children must. We need to know our parents still love each other and cuddle in movie theatres. I hope my dad opens the passenger side door for my mom sometimes when we're not looking. I hope my mom still tells him she loves him, kissing him on the cheek before they go to bed or texting him goodnight when he's on a baseball trip with my brother. I need to know relationships can last.

After the movie, my mom says, "Who is the boy actor?"

I tell her it's Ansel Elgort, the most badass actor on the planet right now (besides Emma Watson and Selena Gomez).

She says, "That boy is magnificent."

I wonder if Ansel Elgort appreciates my mother calling him "magnificent." I recommend my mom write him a letter to tell him how magnificent she thinks he is. I like to think that he would appreciate the letter. If a woman in Ohio understands good acting and knows what a good job he is doing, he has the right to know.

I should write a letter to Emma Watson. For one, a woman who is smart enough and brave enough to stand up for other women across the world about feminism is remarkable. Secondly, the girl is drop-dead gorgeous. I mean, how did two human beings make someone who is that beautiful? She might have been created in a lab with robot genes or something. Thirdly, her accent is TO DIE FOR. Like, I truly get hard while she speaks. But not the kind of hard teenagers get when they see hot girls. Emma Watson isn't hot; she's beautiful. There's a difference. The kind of hard where it erects, but not fully; aroused is a better word. Hot is degrading, but beautiful is special.

Our last activity of the day besides presents and a cake that I'll certainly enjoy is dinner at Applebee's. If it ain't broke, don't fix it. My family has been going to Applebee's ever since I was born. They love it so much and go there so frequently the manager had a picture taken of our family and put up in the kitchen. He showed us one time.

My mother and I always get the "2 for $20" deal. Mozzarella sticks as the appetizer and I always get chicken fingers and she always gets pasta with grilled chicken on the side. She lets me eat her grilled chicken, proving to me how much she loves me.

Dad even lets me get dessert because it's my birthday. Actually, he "lets" me get dessert. My dad and mom told the manager that it was my birthday and the waiters and waitresses came over and sang happy birthday to me the Applebee's way, which is different than the normal happy birthday song. They gave me a free slice of chocolate cake, "on the house." I love the term "on the house." I always feel so special when I get something like that.

Arriving at home is a nice feeling. I'm one step closer to seeing my best friends and the girl I'm in love with. Although I love everything that my parents have done for me, nothing can top being with your friends on your birthday.

I was born at 7:13 p.m. Every year, mom makes sure I blow out the candles at exactly 7:13 p.m. Not a minute before or after. I like this about my mom. It's something special not many families do besides mine. At least, I've asked my friends, and none of their families let them blow out the candles at the exact time they were born. Their parents don't even remember what time they were born.

After making my wish and blowing out the candles, I grab a piece of cake which mom cut for me and take it over to the family room where my brother and dad are watching the Indians play.

"Kluber is on the mound tonight."

"We're gonna win if we get at least two runs."

"C'mon, Kipnis! Hit the ball! It's not that hard!"

Part of me wants to add to their conversation and their yelling. Another part of me doesn't want to go through learning an entire sport in a matter of minutes. The last part of me doesn't care enough to want to try and learn.

Presents are next. After we finish our pieces of cake and watch the Indians beat the Yankees, my dad then lets me to start opening them.

"Fuck the Yankees," my dad says under his breath. My mom tells him to watch his language in front of the kids, like we haven't heard bad language before. But that's who my mom is, always telling my dad to watch his language in front of us. That's another small thing mom does to show her love for me and my brother.

There's only three presents and a poorly handmade card mom made. It says, "To my sweet angel. I will love you to the moon and back for infinity and beyond. Love, Mom," written on the bottom of the card. The infinity and beyond thing is an inside joke between us. Not necessarily a joke, but just my love for *Toy Story*. It's one of the best trilogies ever. I heard they're making a fourth one, and you bet your sweet ass I'm going to the midnight showing.

I open the first present. The anticipation level is nowhere near where it should be because the wrapping slightly gives the present away. I act surprised when I tear the wrapping paper off—a brown, leather baseball glove is in my hands.

"It's from me and your brother," Dad says. He seems proud of the gift I just opened, like an accomplished father. "He's been wanting to play catch with you for a while now. And now you can!" Yippee! How am I supposed to get out of this one?

Trying to match the enthusiasm and excitement my dad and brother have, I say, "Thanks a lot guys! I've been wanting one for a while now. I can see how much you love it, and I'm just glad I have someone to teach me. Someone as good as you anyway." There's at least two lies in what I just said. I don't like to complain when I get gifts, there's no point. Sentimental gifts are nice to receive because the person you get them from is so proud. You don't want to hurt their feelings.

I toss it to the side. I start ripping the poorly wrapped gift with joy on my face. I love making my mother happy. I look down, finishing tearing the wrapping paper to shreds, and the thing that is left in my grasp is a pair of socks with little tiny hula girls dancing in a small bikini. They're placed all over the socks.

Looking at my mom, I yell, "Are you kidding me? I've never seen these before!" That's the truth. I have never, ever, seen this pair of socks before. I don't work at the clown store so where could I have? But mom's face lights up.

"You really like them?" she asks. "I saw how handsome you looked in your suit you wore to church the other day, and these dress socks will complete the outfit." She's wearing the biggest smile on her face. At first, I didn't like the socks, but after hearing the explanation, I love them.

"Thanks so much, Mom," I say, quietly.

She points to the last gift, and I unwrap it quickly, faster than the previous two. I look down in disbelief. A white, shiny Apple Watch in its box.

"You're kidding me," I utter out. I've never seen anything so pretty, Jordyn being excluded. In pure joy and excitement, I jump off my butt and run toward both my parents. "I love you guys," I say, hugging them both. "I don't say it enough."

Mom's heart seems to melt. She falls into my grasp, like an ice cube melting on a sidewalk. Dad doesn't do the same, but I feel him give into the hug too. I can't remember the last time I've hugged my dad before this. Sons don't tend to give hugs to their fathers. It's just an unspoken agreement between father and son. Sometimes, it's needed though. You need to hug your father to realize the love is still there. And for the first time in a long time, I know I love my father. Not the fake love between parent and child, the real kind.

"We love you too, son," dad says sincerely. The first time I've been his son since I've learned how to ride the bike. The time when he was running down the street, pumping his arms in the air. He's been away all summer, but I've realized I've miss him dearly.

An hour later, I leave the house and go over to Jordyn's. The sun is just beginning to set, setting up a perfect end to the perfect day. I didn't know I was going to enjoy the day this much with my family. I speed to Jordyn's and arrive fairly quickly, making sure no laws were broken while driving. I walk around back, avoiding the spots in the grass where new grass is getting filled in. I'm greeted by Nick, Drew, Lindsey, Jordyn, and Jordyn's family, yelling, "SURPRISE!"

Balloons cover the entire perimeter of the yard, tied to the white fence that surrounds the backyard. Two tables with white tulips nicely put in vases are in the middle of the yard. Pictures of me and the rest of the Fantastic Four are hanging from the back of the house and off the gutters, which are filled with leaves and rain water. A crockpot filled with buffalo chicken dip is making the air smell incredible.

They all come running toward me, and a group hug is formed, causing me to lose my breath for a second or two. "I never thought you would make it here," Jordyn says. I am thirty minutes late, and I'm sure Lindsey had a heart attack because, like I said before, she hates it when people are late. But I'm here now, and that's what matters.

We spend the last hour of sunlight sitting at the two tables, eating buffalo chicken dip and telling stories from our childhoods.

Lindsey starts with, "Remember in seventh grade when Julie Hallowell flashed us during trick or treat. She was dressed up as Hermione Granger and wanted a snickers bar so bad, she agreed to flash us if we gave her one. Well worth it."

Then Nick says, "Don't forget about the time when we played the penis game during music in sixth grade. Mr. Siegenthaler really made all four of us go to the office, and they suspended us for three days. Jokes on him because he's gay, and he probably liked us yelling penis at him."

Drew chimes in with, "That one time on the playground where I told Zach Thomas that if he punched me in the face, then I could kick him in the balls. And he punched me in the face and I cried for the rest of the day. But the following day I got my revenge and kicked him in the nut sack so hard I prevented him from having children."

Jordyn finally tells a story, saying, "I remember when flip phones started to become cool and I texted this guy in my class to ask what the homework was, and he sent me a picture of his penis. The first nude I ever received was from Tim Kallas." Jordyn made sure her mother had gone inside before telling her story. But Tiffany, Riley, and Jeff hear it and start cracking up.

"How big?" Riley asks.

Jordyn puts two fingers in the air, which are very close to each other. "Tootsie roll," she says, starting to laugh as soon as the words exit her mouth. Jeff begins rolling on the ground, making the grass stick to his shirt. "Get up!" Jordyn yells at him. And she starts laughing even harder.

When the sunlight dwindles down, causing the sky to turn completely black, Mrs. Wright puts together a fire. It quickly starts to burn the wood and smoke begins to be emitted by the orange and yellow flames. The five of us and Jordyn's family huddle around the fire.

"Thanks a lot, you guys," I say. "This is honestly the best birthday I've ever had."

Drew looks at Nick who looks at Lindsey who looks at Jordyn. "And the evening is far from over," Drew says with a smirk on his face. Something special is planned for me, I can taste it. Unsure if I'm ready for it, I guess I don't have much of a choice.

"What are you guys doing?" Jeff asks. He's like the littler brother I've always wanted. I have a little brother, but not as cool as Jeff. He's the type of brother to roll around the ground when he discovers his sister received a dick pic in seventh grade. My brother is the type of brother who gives baseball mitts as gifts. Very thoughtful and sincere, but not the most ideal brother.

"When you're older," Jordyn says with a big grin on her face. I'm starting to get hot because of the fire. My legs begin to burn, feeling the heat radiate off them. Jordyn's closest to me. She has her arms crossed in front of her, hands tucked beneath her armpits. She seems cold. I suppose the heat isn't hitting her like it's hitting me.

Taking off my jacket, she looks at me and winks. I get up and walk to her, placing it around her shoulders. "Thanks for the jacket, Melon," Jordyn says, adjusting it so it covers her shoulders entirely.

Mrs. Wright and Jeff walk inside and come back a couple minutes later. Mrs. Wright is carrying marshmallows, graham crackers and chocolate bars while Jeff is holding three pairs of shiny metal tongs—the ingredients for s'mores. I've never had s'mores before. I only know these are the ingredients because my brother has watched *The Sandlot* a billion times. It's one of my favorite scenes. That and the scene where Squints kisses Wendy Peffercorn, sucking her lips dry. He is my hero for that scene.

Jeff hands me a pair of tongs, and Mrs. Wright rips opens the bag of marshmallows and throws me one. I surprisingly catch it and place it on my tongs, placing it in the fire. Jordyn and Jeff accompany me, roasting their marshmallows at the same time.

I take mine out and the marshmallow is severely blackened and burnt. I look over to Jordyn and Jeff, their marshmallows looking golden and crisp. "How the heck did you do that?" I ask.

They giggle. "Years of practice," Jeff says. "I once started out blackening my marshmallows like a wee lad like you, my friend." He's not Irish.

"You're not Irish," Jordyn says to him. I knew it. "Don't let him bust your balls, Melon."

I smush it in between two graham crackers, I place the chocolate directly beneath the marshmallow and the chocolate begins to melt as soon as it touches the white, fluffy goodness. I take my first bite, savior the taste, and enjoy it. I'm very glad *The Sandlot* didn't overhype s'mores.

After having four more s'mores, and my stomach begins hurting pretty badly, Jordyn, Nick, Drew and Lindsey tell me it's time to go. "Where are we going?" I ask. But they don't tell me. They say it's another "surprise."

Before thanking the Wrights for everything, I snag another s'more, making Jordyn roast the marshmallow because the past five I've made have all been black. I eat another one very quickly, then thank Mrs. Wright, Tiffany, Riley, and Jeff. I thank Mrs. Wright for allowing Jordyn to throw this party at the house and the buffalo chicken dip. I thank Tiffany for being such a nice sister to Jordyn and looking like her. I thank Riley for staying off her phone for most of the night and laughing at my bad jokes. And I thank Jeff for thinking that Jordyn's seventh grade love story involving the dick pic was as hilarious as I did. And for bringing out the tongs that made the delicious s'mores.

We pile in Jordyn's car to go to the mysterious place which reminds me of the time Jordyn took me to the waterfall. I can see everything this time, though, which I'm very thankful for. Nick says, "Get ready for the time of your life," which makes me very eager for us to get started.

On the way there, I continue to thank them for such an amazing birthday, which makes them very frustrated.

"We get it. You're thankful. You're happy. This is the best birthday ever," Nick tries to say in his best impression of me. It's very bad because he didn't get the pitch right. My voice is higher than his impression implied.

Drew turns on Twenty-One Pilots, but I tell him to let Jordyn choose the music because I'm not interested in hearing that type of music for the night. So Jordyn plugs her phone into the aux and turns on a song that is very peaceful. It's country and called "Friends In Low Places." It's by a man named Garth Brooks who I imagine growing old with his wife and spitting tobacco into a metal bucket while singing to his wife on the front porch of their one floored home.

"WE'RE HERE!" yells Lindsey after minutes go by of "Friends in Low Places" and other country songs. I don't recognize the area. It's an open field with trees and shrubs placed sporadically throughout. A police station is on the opposite side of the field, where few cop cars are parked in a parking lot. It's a Thursday night, so not many cops should be roaming the town. It seems like they are though due to the small number of cars that are actually parked at the police station.

Jordyn begins to slow down, making the brakes squeal until we finally stop. The four of them get out of the car, me following closely behind them. My heart racing, not knowing what is coming next. What could we possibly do in an open field by a police station.

"Is it still a secret?" I ask. They all shush me, raising their index fingers to their lips.

"No, it's not," whispers Jordyn. "But you have to be quiet now. We're going to have a little fun on your eighteenth birthday. What time is it?"

Lindsey pulls her phone out and looks at it. "11:50."

"Perfect," Jordyn says. "Okay, if you must know. We're about to streak the hallow."

"*Streak*?" I ask. They shush me again but I thought I said it quietly enough. I guess not. "Like, get-naked-and-run-as-fast-as-we-can sort of streaking?" I ask in a quieter tone of voice.

They all nod. Even Drew seems excited to streak. I'm the only hesitant one, which means I'm the only one who's thinking logically We walk over to a tree, which is a couple steps off the road. The field must be at least 100 yards in length. I'm being forced to run the length of a football field while my nuts and penis flop around, causing me intense pain.

"Before we get started," Jordyn begins. "There is one goal we all have to accomplish during our streaking adventure. We all, and I can't stress this enough, we *all* have to put our ass on the front door of the police station. It's the only thing we have to do."

All the faces that were just filled with excitement turn to faces filled with terror. "We have to put our bare ass on the front door of the police station?" asks Lindsey. "Is that smart?"

"Obviously, no," Jordyn whispers. "But it's really exhilarating and fun. You'll never feel more alive in your entire life. Okay?"

"Okay," I say. Then Drew says okay. Then Lindsey. Then Nick. We all agree to Jordyn's horrible idea. We begin stripping our clothes off, beginning with our shirts. Jordyn is still wearing my jacket, so I was cold prior to my shirt being taken off. My nipples are extremely hard, and I hope no one notices.

I fall down while attempting to balance myself, trying to take off my pants now. Instead, I take them off while sitting down, making my underwear soaking wet due to the dew on the grass. Everyone is in their underwear at this point. Jordyn has a white bra and white underwear on. She's the only person I look at in their underwear. Getting caught by the police is no longer the scariest thing tonight; getting a boner in front of Jordyn surpasses it as my number one fear.

"On the count of three?" Jordyn asks. "We take our underwear off. One... Two... Three!"

The five of us take our underwear off, revealing the parts we've never seen before. "The unknown." I catch a quick glimpse of Jordyn's right boob before she uses her arm to block them from my sight. Her titty, looking perfect for the one second I saw it. She uses her left hand to cover her vagina from my sight as well.

I don't think I should feel bad for looking. Hell, who wouldn't look? But a little guilt runs through me. She hasn't given me permission to look at her naked, yet here I am. I don't want to apologize for it though because I don't think she saw me looking.

We throw all of our clothes and phones and wallets underneath the big tree. I look in front of me, seeing nothing but grass, trees, shrubs, and a police station. Their front door is about to be bombarded with five teenage asses. Some pretty, some not so pretty.

"Now. On the count of three. We begin the extravagant adventure of a lifetime. No turning back and no slowing down. One... Two... Three!"

BAM! We take off. Wind flowing through my hair and making my penis even smaller than it usually is. I run through holes in the ground, making my feet ache in pain. Jordyn, right beside me, is running as fast as she can, avoiding the holes in the ground, looking like she has done this before. Her hands and arms remain over her boobs and vagina. Nick is in the lead amongst us, running a lot quicker than I expected him to. Lindsey and Drew are side by side, behind me and Jordyn. I decide to drop back a little further, acting like I'm getting tired. Jordyn speeds ahead of me, her butt is moving up and down. Side to side. Round and perfect. I hope this doesn't' make me a pervert, wanting to see the ass of the girl I'm in love with.

When I reach Drew and Lindsey, we're about halfway through the open field. I suddenly notice red-and-blue flashing lights driving down the road and stopping directly behind our car. I say as loudly as I can, not trying to be heard by the cops, "Guys. The cops are by our car." Jordyn hears me and dead sprints up to Nick. We all stop.

My feet feel like they're in quick sand, not being able to move. My heart, pumping blood faster and faster and faster, feels like it's about to burst out of my chest. My adrenaline is at an all-time high, making the pain in my feet vanish. I feel no pain, only fear. Fear of being arrested on my eighteenth birthday.

Collecting my thoughts for a couple seconds, I finally will myself to run behind a bush, dragging my feet with me. The other four decide to follow my lead and quickly, without even thinking, the five of us are on our hands and knees, hiding from the cops, behind a fucking shrub. Flashlights are peaking from behind the tree where we stripped our clothes off from our bodies. Lights are being flashed on our clothes, and they soon begin making their way down the field, realizing there are naked people streaking the hallow. But not knowing there are naked teenagers streaking the hallow. Teenagers that are not looking to go to jail tonight.

"I have to pee," Nick whispers, very quietly even I can barely hear him and I'm directly next to him.

"Now is really not the best time," I say to him. For a moment, I forget we're all naked. If a camera came and took a picture of us at this very instant, it would capture five naked teenagers on their hands and knees hiding behind a bush. Now that, would be a picture that will be in the yearbook.

"I really have to," and he ever so slightly crawls away from us. I look behind me and see a tree where Nick is crawling toward. He stands up, trying not to make any noise and pees. The sound of urine hitting the tree and smacking the dirt beneath cannot be unheard and is marked in my everlasting memory.

Looking at the shining light pointed in our direction, I switch my focus to Jordyn, who's directly beside me. "What's the plan?"

She looks as confused as I do. "No idea," she whispers. "I'm going to follow you." She's trusting me, in full nudity and all. In danger of getting caught by the police, she puts all her trust on me. Oh shit.

I begin to panic, like I'm not already. Ideas flowing through my brain. Do we run toward the police station? No, clearly no. Do we run for our car and past the cops? No way. I move my focus to the right where I see a house far in the distance. The trees appear to be blocking the house from the cops.

I wave my hand, trying to grasp the attention of everyone else. Nick, who is finally finished with his pee, comes crawling back toward the pack. I hope he didn't put his knee in the puddle of piss next to the tree. I point my hand to the direction of the house. I count down with my fingers from three. No talking. Two. Without hesitation. One.

I start sprinting toward the house. I look back and see four naked teenagers following me. Only four naked teenagers, no cops. Slowing down just enough to reach Jordyn, I grab her hand. She stops covering her breasts with that hand and grabs it back. Her fingers intertwined with mine, running naked in a field away from cops with three other naked friends—the ideal date.

We continue sprinting. Left. Right. Left. Right. Looking back every so often and seeing no cops chasing us. Dodging trees that cross our path, Jordyn pulling me toward her, me pulling Jordyn toward me, trying our best to avoid holes in the ground so we don't have to make a stop to the ER.

The house is becoming bigger and bigger. The moonlight appears to be shining down on the house, like it's our final destination after years of traveling. We're far from our clothes and far from the police station. Even better, far from the cops that were once directly on top of us.

We're right by the house now. A car parked in the driveway, looking like the perfect hiding spot for five naked teenagers running from the cops. We run around the car and sit down, all five of us breathing as heavily as we ever breathed before. Jordyn's and my hands are no longer intertwined, but resting on the ground.

"Good eyes," Drew says. He needs to get into better shape. He can barely breathe at this point.

"Much appreciated," I say in return. "Now. We can't wake up the people that live here. We just need to wait out the cops and get our clothes and get out of here. ASAP."

August 4, 2017

1 2:00 a.m. The dark sky is making it hard to see Jordyn's naked body. Luckily, the dark sky is making it hard to see Drew and Nick and Lindsey's body as well. My eighteenth birthday is finally over. What started with a nice breakfast at my favorite restaurant ended with hiding behind a stranger's car, naked with my best friends.

"How long should we wait?" Jordyn asks. "My butt is getting extremely dirty."

I laugh. Not the loudest laugh, but a decent one. "That should be the last of your worries," I tell her.

"How was your pee?" Lindsey asks Nick. "You seriously couldn't have waited five minutes?"

"No, I couldn't have. Besides, I was looking at the cops. They weren't even close to us."

Creeping to the end of the sidewalk, I look down the road to spot no cop car. The only car I see is Jordyn's. With our luck, the cops probably decided to take our clothes and phones and wallets to the station. They know exactly who we are, and they'll arrest us as soon as we walk through those doors to retrieve our stuff. That's the worst-case scenario.

I motion the four of them to come near me. "I think the coast is clear," I whisper. "Everyone catch their breath?" Suddenly, a light in one of the upstairs rooms flashes on. Without hesitating, I race my way to our clothes. Hearing heavy breathing behind me, I know the others are following my lead, hopefully not looking back at the house.

We begin to slow down when we get close to our car. It's too dark to see if our clothes remain underneath the tree from this distance. I stop running and start walking, holding my arms above my head to get some oxygen flowing through my body. For not running since freshman year of high school, I was moving relatively quick.

Slowly, I walk up to the tree. Our clothes are there, along with our phones and wallets. The cops have left and it's almost like nothing had happened the past ten minutes.

"Get dressed everyone," I say sternly. "There will be no asses being put on front doors tonight." The rest agree and put their clothes on.

My underwear is still damp from sitting on the grass. I slip my socks and shoes on after I fully get dressed and wait for the others. Lindsey is the last one to be ready, claiming it's "a lot tougher for women to get dressed because of the bra." I understand, but they should be used to it by now.

Our heads hanging low, we walk toward the car in displeasure, knowing we didn't accomplish the only goal we had. Everyone is tired from the marathon we had just run and no one talks for a while, trying to process what had just happened.

After minutes of silence, Drew yells, "That was insane!" He sticks his head out the window, yelling at the top of his lungs. "WE'RE FUGITIVES! COME CATCH US YOU FILTHY PIGS!"

I can't believe we just ran from the cops.

"What just happened?" Jordyn says. "I mean… What the heck just happened?"

Singing every song on the way home, we reminisce what it felt like to run naked and run from the flashlights that were being held by two cops. The feeling of freedom we had just experienced and the way we just lived.

"And to think," Lindsey begins, "we're not even done with the night!"

Not even done? How much more can they have planned? I don't want to know what I'm about to do or about to endure. It's only right they do not tell me. I'm just happy to be sitting in the same car with these weirdos.

We enter the city of Delaware, which is very close to Worthington, but much different. There's a lot more farmland in Delaware than there is in Worthington; lots of cows and sheep and goats. I've only driven through Delaware, making my opinion invalid. It's just what I've heard around town.

Jordyn parks her car next to a strip of small shops on the side of the road. There aren't many cars lining the streets at 12:30 a.m., maybe three or four joining ours. We walk into a shop that says, "OPEN" on the window. Jordyn tells me I'm not allowed to look above the door, which would "spoil the surprise."

It's dark and cold. What kind of shop would be open at 12:30 on a Thursday night? Twelve-thirty on a Friday morning I suppose is the correct term now. I don't see a counter and can't smell alcohol, so it isn't a bar. No racks filled with clothes so it's nothing like that. A scary man wearing a black t-shirt with no writing walks up to us, tattoos covering his arms. All different kinds of tattoos including pictures of people's faces, animals, crosses, and the list can go on and on. I know where we are—a tattoo parlor.

"Hi there," Jordyn says to the scary man. He's not creepy like the guy at the bowling alley, but a six-foot-five-inch ball of iron weighing at least 300 pounds, the stereotypical man who works at a tattoo parlor at 12:30 a.m.

"My friend here would like to get a tattoo tonight," she points to me. I try hiding behind Nick, but he moves out of the way. My mother would kill me if I get a tattoo.

"What do you want?" The man asks, his voice higher than anticipated, not matching his size.

I stutter, "I-I haven't really thought about it. Do you recommend any?"

"I'll give you a couple minutes," and he walks away, leaving the five us to come up with ideas for a tattoo I'll be receiving tonight.

"Are you kidding me, guys?" I say to them in an angry tone. "I mean, c'mon! A tattoo? I can't even donate blood at the school blood drive. How am I supposed to endure the pain of a needle piercing my skin repeatedly for an hour?"

"Get a small one," Nick says. "At least that way it's not an hour worth of pain. It's like thirty minutes of pain." He winks at me after saying this.

133

"You're more than welcome to get one, too, dick." I'm a little frightened to tell the truth. I've never even considered getting a tattoo. The thought of them just never appealed to me; having something on your body forever. I don't get it. Plus, the pain aspect. I bawled after getting a splinter in middle school.

I think of what I can get. What makes sense? Dragon on my arm, no. Snake slithering across my entire body, God no. A cross to pay tribute for a loved one? Well, I don't even know when my grandmother's birthday is, so no. Then, I start thinking, what makes me, me? I have no special characteristics unique to me. Nothing that pops out to people or shows people who I am.

But tattoos aren't used to show people who you are. Tattoos are only special to the person receiving it. It doesn't matter what people think about it; it only matters what I think of it. The one thing that shapes me into the person I am. The one thing that defines me and no one will ever notice. The conversation with Jordyn when I first met her. The sincerity in her voice. The way she sat and talked with me, listening when I spoke. She could have gotten up and left with her friends, but rather sat with me and understood my *Star Wars* reference and genuinely seemed like she cared about people like me.

"I'm ready!" I yell out to the scary man.

Everyone is excited but confused at the same time. "What are you going to get?" Nick asks.

"Something special," I answer, a smile resting on my face. I'm no longer scared, but eager to get a tattoo. I've never thought about something that's special enough to be on my body for the rest of my life. A symbol could never define me. But this one is as close as it gets.

The man, whose legs are skinny, guides me to a chair that's in the back of the store. I can't believe I'm about to get a tattoo from a man whose store is open at 12:30 a.m. It's probably some store on the black market. In exchange for tattoos, they expect drugs or alcohol. I'm almost positive that's how the black market works.

I tell the man what I want, not letting Jordyn or anybody else know. Jordyn is the only one who comes back with me and the rest stay and sit in the broken-down chairs and couches which is called the "visiting area." Jordyn holds my hand as the man begins giving me the tattoo, the sharp needle piercing my skin. I'm not going to lie, it hurts, a lot. I squeeze Jordyn's hand while I sweat profusely, making her hand soaking sweat.

"Sorry," I mumble, clenching my teeth because of the pain.

"Don't be. Everything is going to be fine. It's going to turn out great."

The sense of security while I'm with her is something I've never felt before. I believe her when she says everything is going to be fine. I'm not sure if it's how she says it or what, but I believe her.

I decide to get it directly below my shoulder on my arm, which can't be seen while still wearing a short-sleeved t-shirt. I don't want to look at it before he's finished, so I keep my eyes on Jordyn. Seeing it for the first time when it's finished is going to be well worth it.

About fifteen minutes later, he tells me he's finished. Jordyn is still holding my sweaty hand, and I didn't cry once, not one drop. I imagined myself crying in the chair when I found out I was getting a tattoo when we walked through the door with the pain would intensifying as time went by. But I didn't. I can't cry in front of Jordyn.

"Don't look at it yet, Jord," I tell her. I want to be the first one to see it, it's only right. Closing my eyes, I turn my head and look down at my right arm. Very slowly, I open. And before me, I see a tattoo. On me, a tiny slice of watermelon with "Watermelon Guy" in cursive writing directly beneath it. It's small, but big at the same time. Not like Times New Roman, 12-point font like every teacher wants their papers; bigger than that.

"I love it," I say, smiling from ear to ear. I really do love it. "Jordyn, look."

She turns her head and looks at my arm, a big smile spreads across her face. Jordyn faces the man and yells: "This is great!" Even the scary man with the big upper body and stick legs smiles. "Melon! I'm so proud of you, man! This is incredible! A real tattoo!"

I understand her excitement, but she really needs to stop yelling, it's beginning to hurt my ears.

I wave to the other three. "Guys, come check it out."

They come rushing into the back of the tattoo parlor and stare at my arm. Their eyes are in amazement and Nick says, "That's awesome, man."

Lindsey adds, "So proud of you *Melon.*" She winks at me.

And Drew says, "Incredible, dude. Really manly."

It doesn't matter if it's manly or not because I'm happy about it. I'm happy to be a watermelon guy, both figuratively and literally. I love watermelon. I prefer it over any other fruit. "How much is it?" I ask the man.

"Don't worry about it, buddy," he answers. "I can see how scared you were. And your buddies told me it was your birthday present. So happy birthday, bud." What a nice guy.

"Holy cow, man. Thanks a lot."

"You got it. Just be sure to apply this stuff on every couple hours. About three times a day for the next few." He hands me a bottle. It appears to be some sort of petroleum jelly. Not sure what it does, but I don't want my tattoo to sting so looks like I have to apply this stuff.

Thanking him again, Jordyn leads the way out the door and jumps into the driver's seat. I follow her and toss myself into the back seat, letting Lindsey sit up front. Even though we're celebrating my birthday, the girls should have an opportunity for girl talk if they choose to do so.

Before we drive away from the sketchy, yet very cleaned up tattoo parlor, Lindsey says, "Last stop is a two-parter, Melon. Same location but two different tasks to accomplish. You up for it?"

"Heck yeah," I say back. I think I'm showing Jordyn I can have conversations without cussing. I've been doing a fairly good job watching my mouth around her.

I pull out my phone and look at the time. 1:30 a.m. My parents are probably shitting their pants at the moment, so I decide to text them saying I'm okay and having fun with my friends. Instantly, mom texts back:

> Thanks for letting me know. Have fun.
> Love you.

Getting that out of the way, I slip my phone back into my pocket, gearing up for the last stop of a long night. It's a quick trip to the last location, making the song choices crucial. Drew forces Jordyn to let him play a song, which turns out to be "Ode to Sleep," by Twenty-One Pilots. Not a bad one, but predictable. Having time for one more, Jordyn took back the aux cord and plays "Fast Car" by Tracy Chapman. Slow and fast, a great choice.

I get out of the car, surprised to see our local grocery store. "What are we doing here?" I ask.

"You'll see," Jordyn says, smirking. Walking into the grocery store, we don't go toward the food but make a quick left. I soon figure out why we're here.

"Okay," Drew starts, "Do you want to go big and play the Mega Millions or go small and buy some scratch offs?" There's not many things in life that are guaranteed, but one of them is losing the Mega Millions lottery. So I like my chances with the scratch off. I move toward the big red machine that reminds me of a vending machine, but instead sweet treats are replaced with precious opportunities to win big money.

Although tattoos never appealed to me, the lottery always did. My parents never wanted to play while I was growing up because they thought it would "set a bad example" for my brother and me. Dad always said, "People who play the lottery are either, one, addicted to drugs; two, have no money, or three, addicted to drugs and have no money." I don't think there's any truth in that.

The thought of winning always made me want to play. Losing never crossed my mind, except for the Mega Millions. If you lose, you've just wasted a couple bucks. Low risk, high reward.

I slide $5 into the slot and it sucks up my money. I push a button that says, "Quick Cash" across the top of it. It's $5 with a chance to win $1000—seems like easy money to me. A couple seconds letter, a tiny piece of paper appears from the bottom of the machine, a receipt quickly following.

"Anyone have a penny or something?" I ask the group, patting down my pockets searching for one.

"Use your fingernail, pussy," Lindsey says. And I do because I don't want Lindsey to think of me as a pussy, although she knows

I am one. To win, all I need to do is scratch off three $1000 boxes. Easy enough. There's nine boxes total on the card so three of those being $1000's seems likely.

I'm wrong. I scratch off all nine, only finding two $1000 boxes in the process. I am quickly finding out what my parents were talking about. I might as well have tossed my $5 in the wind. Winning appears so easy, which makes it look so intriguing. All you have to do is find three numbers that match up. But actually finding three boxes that match up and read the same number—borderline impossible.

"Sorry, dude," Nick says, a poor attempt of trying to seem sincere. "On the bright side, there's one more thing you're legally allowed to do tonight." He starts jumping up and down.

Is legally buying cigarettes worth Nick's jumping like a school girl? Absolutely not. I'll let him have his fun, I suppose. We walk over to the poor woman who's working at Kroeger very early on a Friday. I really hope she doesn't have any kids because she wouldn't have had the chance to tuck them in tonight. And what time will she get off? Can she put them on the school bus tomorrow morning? I'll feel terrible if she can't.

"How are you doing?" I ask the woman who's slouching behind the counter. She seems miserable, like nothing in the world has a prayer of making her feel better.

"Terrific. Yourself?" Lie. She doesn't have to lie to me. I'll understand completely if she says she was doing terrible.

"Superb, thanks. Can I have a box of cigarettes please?"

"What kind?"

"Surprise me." I didn't know there were multiple kinds of cigarettes. I just thought there were the bad kind that kill you.

She leaves for a second and immediately comes back, holding a box of cigarettes. "$5.25."

"Don't you need to see my ID?" I ask. It kind of defeats the purpose if she doesn't want to see my ID.

"I believe you're eighteen kid," she says. Her tone is getting progressively grouchier as she continues to speak.

"Take my ID. I swear I'm eighteen." I hand it to her. I really want her to check me and not believe I'm legal age to purchase cigarettes; it's more fun this way. Besides, I had my ID out of my wallet and ready to hand her since we got out of the car. I had a suspicion that's why we came to Kroger.

She snatches it out of my hand and glances it over, skimming over it quickly. "Happy belated birthday, kid," she says. Then I hand her $20, telling to keep the change. I want her family to have breakfast for the next couple days. Working at Kroeger cannot possibly pay the bills and allow her children to eat breakfast; it just can't.

Walking out, Jordyn says, "All right, let's smoke them bad boys." She's serious too.

"Uh, I'll pass," I say. "I thought the point of us coming her was for me to buy them, not to smoke them.

"Well, dude," Nick says, "then you will be wasting that money too." That's funny to me because he was one of the reasons I played the lottery. He is talking like it was my idea to lose $5.

"I don't want to get lung cancer and die before I reach twenty. I have a lot to live for."

Lindsey pulls a lighter out of her pocket. "Sorry, man. There's no getting out of this one. I stole this from my dad, risking my life for you. The least you can do is relax and share a cigarette with your best friends."

I give in. Smoking once won't force me to lose a couple years on my life. It'll just give me another story to tell my children.

After tearing open the box, I open it and offer cigarettes to my fellow peers, who all seem strangely eager to get started. With the skinny white objects of death in between our fingers, Lindsey walks around lighting the bottoms of the cigarettes.

"Okay," Jordyn says. "My sister says it's a quick breath and puff. Don't inhale."

"Doesn't breathing involve inhaling?" I ask, but no answer. Lindsey finishes lighting everyone's cigarettes and we raise our hands.

"To an unforgettable night and this bitch's eighteenth birthday," Drew says. We raise our cigarettes in the air, quickly pretending to hit them on a table and then lift our hands to our mouths. A quick breath is all I do. In the process, I mistakenly inhale on accident and begin coughing. We all do though, every single one of us coughing. It's actually quite funny.

I'm still coughing when Jordyn says, "This was a horrible idea!" And she continues coughing. After a minute or two, the coughing dies down and turns into laughter. An eruption of laughter fills the empty parking lot, where five teenagers who had just made their first critical, life-altering decision. A bit dramatic, but still true.

Simultaneously, we throw the cigarettes down and put the toe of our shoes on them, causing the cigarette to extinguish, just like everyone does in the movies, allowing me to feel like I'm John Travolta in *Grease*. "Remind me to never do that again," I say.

"We had to do it once," Jordyn adds. "I agree, though." Then we pile back into Jordyn's car. She begins dropping everyone off at their houses, starting with Nick. Then goes Drew and then Lindsey, leaving me last. Just like I want her to. Of course, I thank everyone for a good night before they get out, all echoing the same response, "Stop thanking me."

I move into the passenger seat when she finally drops Lindsey off, accidently hitting Jordyn in the face, making her say, "Watch yourself, Melon," in dramatic fashion.

Knowing she is kidding, I say, "You're lucky it wasn't harder." Which isn't funny, but Jordyn giggles anyway, causing me to smile. "I had a great time tonight."

"I'm glad you did," she says back.

"It's because of you to be completely honest." The mood seems to shift. Laughing and joking quickly changes into something serious. This is the time. I'm going to tell her how I feel. I'm putting myself out there.

"Stop, Melon. It was all of us. Everyone had a part in it." She's being modest. I know the other shitheads had nothing to do with tonight. Jordyn hosted the party and had gone streaking before. Lindsey is the only other person who is eighteen besides Jordyn, and I know she hasn't purchased a lottery ticket or even considered smoking. That just leaves the tattoo and I assume that was her idea as well.

"No, please stop. You're amazing, Jordyn. Don't try to be modest." I'm being serious. Suddenly, nerves filter through my body. I've never told someone how I feel before. I knew I would have to if I ever wanted a girlfriend but didn't know it would be a girl like Jordyn. I didn't quite get how much I could like a girl until I met her. How insanely mad I am about someone. Knowing she's the girl I would want to meet my parents. Realizing I want the best for her. I want to compliment and spoil her. I want to walk in public and have people stare at me, asking, "Why is she with you? She's way too attractive to be with you." And I wouldn't take offense because I know it's the truth.

"Thanks, Melon. You're the best," she says, seeming like she means it. Her voice, soft, almost forcing me to jump into her arms. Moments go by without either of us saying anything. Music isn't playing, making the silence deafening. Anxiety fills my body, causing me to second guess whether I should tell her my feelings toward her.

When Jordyn pulls in the driveway, I concluded to not tell her. I don't want to screw up the relationship we've built this summer. I care for her, more than I've ever cared for a single soul in my entire life. And having that feeling be diminished after telling her how I feel and her not feeling the same way would kill me. It would be like a nightmare turned into reality.

She turns off the car. "I've never felt more alive than I did tonight," I say wholeheartedly, hoping she can hear the sincerity in my voice. "And I really like your car." I hadn't told her that yet. It is a nice car, even though I can't name it.

"It's only temporary," she says, with a smug look on her face. "This is the car before the car. Only for the brief amount of time before I'm able to buy a better one. My dad always told me his number one goal in life, excluding the whole marriage-and-kids lovey, gooey stuff was to own a really nice car."

"And that would be what?"

"A gorgeous-looking Lambo, just for Sundays."

I've never really thought about buying a nice car that looks gorgeous. People only want nice stuff to be able and show it off. Buying nice things is just an excuse to start a conversation with someone who fake cares about the nice thing you bought. But I'm glad Jordyn has this idea because it gives her something to work toward.

A couple seconds go by with silence filling up the car. "It was a really fun night," she says, eventually, breaking the silence, turning her head looking at me. She sounds different now, changing her tone from only a few moments ago. Almost as if she's on the verge of tears.

"Are you okay?" I ask her, putting my hand on her shoulder. It's awkward at first, reaching for her shoulder. But she knows I'm trying to comfort her. All I want to do when she isn't feeling well is to comfort her.

"I'm fine, don't worry." She sinks into her car seat, relieving her tension. "You know how much I care for you right?" Oh, no, the conversation that never ends well.

"Of course, I do."

"I don't want to hurt you. Ever. That's the last thing I ever want to do in this world is to hurt you." Why is she saying this? She doesn't have to say this. I should kiss her, but then it'll feel rushed. I don't want our first kiss to feel rushed. Do I hear her out or run? My first instinct is to run.

"I care for you more than I cared for Elliot. More than I cared for any of my boyfriends to be honest. I'm just not ready to start anything. I need to continue to put my trust in God before I put my trust in anyone else."

The air is cool, even with the car off. No lights are on outside my house. With my eyes adjusted, I can see her begin to cry. Not sobbing like the one day at the waterfall, but one or two tears come rolling off her cheek. With my hand still resting on her shoulder, I slide forward, maybe an inch of space separating us now. "I would never hurt you."

She lowers her head, taking her eyes off me. "I know you would never purposely hurt me."

I've heard enough of this shit. "You deserve everything in this life, Jordyn. Everything you can think of, you *deserve*. So don't think of yourself as anything less than enough because that's exactly what you are. You're the most amazing person I know, truly. And I apologize if I'm rambling but you just need to realize how special you are to people in your life." And then I say one more thing. There's not a sound in the neighborhood, there's not a sound in the city, I wouldn't be able to hear a fucking nuke land on my driveway. In this moment, I lean into her, our foreheads touching and whisper, "You would *never*, ever, hurt me."

Jordyn retreats, just a little. I see her eyes staring into mine, appearing as crystal clear as I've seen. I could notice her eyes if it were pitch black and I was an old blind man in a sea of people. Her eyes are that special, that visible, that *real*. She then comes inching forward, just enough to lay a tiny kiss on my cheek, keeping her lips there for a few seconds. This moment, this soon-to-be memory, will never be forgotten.

I don't want to make her regret anything. Her mind is made, and I know I can't convince her otherwise. I respect her decision, truly. If she's not ready, she just isn't. She can't control the timing of when she wants a boyfriend or not. It's been less than a month since Elliot cheated on her. Less than *one* month. She can't rush into anything without knowing what she really wants.

And I'm sure as hell not going to push her away by trying to pursue something that isn't quite there. She'll feel the same way about me soon, if she doesn't already. I know it.

"This is one of the many things I love about you," I say. She's crying because she isn't ready to have me. "You do everything in life, trying not to hurt anyone."

"I can't live with myself otherwise," she says, leaning back into her chair, her eyes staring at me once again. "I just don't want you to be mad at me."

"Never. I'll never be mad at you."

"You're the best, Jaxson."

Epiphany: Happiest moment of my life.

The waterfall is just as beautiful the second time than it is the first. Jordyn swooped me from my house after her Bible study, complaining the entire car ride how "young and stupid" everyone is. They "don't trust God the way they should." It's late when she picked me up, making the waterfall very buggy. I try to avoid the bugs from getting in my eyes and mouth, but to no avail.

Not swimming at all, we sit on the rock where she told me about her father passing. The same rock she opened up to me for the first time. She acts the same way she did before telling me there won't be an *us* anytime soon. Which clearly hurts, but the idea that there could be an *us* provides hope.

The sound of the water is calming, reminding me of a summer vacation me and my family took a couple years ago. I was laying on the beach, listening to the crashing of the waves. This family next to ours was playing country music through this big, loud speaker. It was too loud for me to hear anyone else around me, but not loud enough to be annoying, the perfect volume.

One song played that I haven't forgotten. It was called "She's Everything" by a guy named Brad Paisley, who's very talented. I had to ask my dad who sang the song. The crashing of the waves was cancelled out by the sound of his voice. It was so deep and soft. Before hearing that song, I didn't know the combination of deep and soft was achievable.

I memorized the song that day. I closed my eyes and tried to remember the words while it was playing. I knew most of them before leaving the beach, replaying the song all day in my head. One day, I would want a girl that meant so much to me like that girl meant to Brad Paisley. Thinking about it sitting on the rocks, hip to hip with the most beautiful girl in the world, realizing I've found the girl in the song, I play the song in my head:

> She's a Saturday out on the town
> And a church girl on Sunday
> She's a cross around her neck
> And a cuss word cause it's Monday
> She's a bubble bath and candles
> Baby, come and kiss me
> She's a one glass of wine
> And she's feeling kinda tipsy
> She's the giver I wish I could be
> And the stealer of the covers
> She's a picture in my wallet
> Of my unborn children's mother
> She's the hand that I'm holding
> When I'm on my knees and praying
> She's the answer to my prayer
> And she's the song that I'm playing

Since that summer, I've known I want a girl like this. And just now, finally realizing, I've discovered my dream girl. Sitting on a rock with bugs flying into your nose and ears, nearly impossible to feel comfortable. But, I am comfortable. Understanding I'm next to her, and can't possibly get *more* comfortable

She keeps complaining about her Bible study. "I don't know what's worse," she says. "Not learning about God or playing games while learning about God." Honestly, it makes no sense why they have to play so many games. It's Bible study, not fucking recess.

She keeps talking, but the singing of the birds takes over. Jordyn stops, listening to their chirping. Crickets chime in, sounding like they're trying to communicate with the birds, which I know isn't possible, but it's quite an idea that certain animals can speak with other animals. I would like to think of it as girls like Jordyn eating watermelons instead of apples. Sometimes you need to talk with people you're not normally used to talking to.

I begin wondering why Elliot cheated on Jordyn. Looking at her, you can't notice a single flaw about her appearance. Hair is wavy, not curly nor straight. Her cheeks are always rosy, but not red. She's not skinny, which I respect her for—Jordyn doesn't miss any meals. She doesn't watch what she eats and her appreciation for ice cream is damn near as much as the next person. But don't get me wrong, Jordyn is not fat.

"I wrote my summer English assignment about this place," I tell her. I was going to wait for Jordyn to ask about it, but I couldn't wait any longer.

"Oh yeah? Can I read it?"

"Of course," I say. "I'll give it to you in the next couple days."

We go home soon after. Jordyn has me drive because the long walk forces her to take a nap on the way back. With the vents blowing cold air in our faces, she rests her legs on the dashboard, reclining her chair all the way back. I don't turn on the radio, deciding it would wake her up. Instead, I drive the whole way back, listening to the deep breaths while she sleeps, her body rising and falling with every breath. Thank god for GPS, because there was no way I would get home without it, especially because I was blindfolded the first time I came out here.

August 9, 2017

Lindsey introduces me to her new girlfriend, Hannah. She explains to me Hannah is the mall girl that Jordyn and her met while wandering. She's tall and has blonde hair, resembling the bright sun. I'm surprised not by how pretty she is, but her bowling abilities—beating Lindsey with a score of 260, very impressive. Lindsey's personal best is only 245.

I know she's good at bowling because she understands how to keep score; it's very complicated. Hannah attempts to explain them to me, but no luck. Me trying to learn how to keep score in bowling is equivalent to trying to teach a dog how to speak English.

The creepy man with the mustache has turned into the creepy man with no mustache. I'm very disappointed after he reveals himself when I go to return my shoes. I only recognize him because he is hesitant to speak with Lindsey. All that time we thought it was Lindsey's feet almost killing him, but he actually has epilepsy. He told me after Lindsey says:, "Wise, very wise," after not placing the shoes in a cubby, but throwing them, acting like they're a hot potato.

Hannah and Lindsey say goodbye and drive away in Hannah's car, which is very nice. Pretty and rich, not sure how Lindsey's gaydar was triggered when she met her, but happy it was because Lindsey needs a girlfriend. She deserves one.

I ask Jordyn if she has any plans for dinner and she responds in a sarcastic tone, "I think me and Michelle Obama have plans tonight. I'm sorry, but when Michelle calls, I must attend."

Laughing, I fake punch her, trying to be funny myself. But I'm not good at making jokes. Yet again, Jordyn laughs though, making me feel good about myself.

"Do you want to come over for dinner?" I ask her after the laughter dies down. "I think my mother would really love to meet you."

She tenses up, her eyes avoiding mine. "You think that's a good idea?" she asks. "I get really nervous around parents. I never know what to say and I suck at making small talk."

I laugh again. "Jordyn, she's going to think you're incredible. You put up with me every day so you're already doing something right. Tell her what a great son she's made. Parents love that."

"Didn't you tell my mother what a great job she did raising me?" I wink at her and a grin appears on her face "Fine. But I'm telling you that small talk is not my forte. And it's not a date, do not get the wrong idea." It's totally a date. Two love birds and a mom.

Pulling in the driveway a couple minutes later, Jordyn follows me in the front door. I sense her nerves when she's behind me, her breaths quick and her steps slow, as if she's debating on what's the best opening line she's going to lead off with.

"Mom!" I yell. "I brought my friend over for dinner. I hope that's okay."

A few seconds later, I hear pounding down the steps. Running quickly, trying to lay eyes on the mystery guest, my mom comes swooping into the kitchen where both me and Jordyn are standing, snacking on little tiny pretzels with peanut butter in the middle, the best damn snack in the world.

Looking shocked, she murmurs out words that are barely able to get made out. Her mouth barely changes, staying opening and hardly moving. "Hello, I'm Mom, but please call me Susan." She throws her hand out, expecting Jordyn to shake it.

Jordyn goes in for a hug instead, opening her arms wide and closing the distance between them. "I'm Jordyn," she says. "You have raised a wonderful son, Susan. He really is one of a kind." Atta girl, Jordyn. Perfect start.

The hugging stops and Mom retreats. Her mouth is closed now, but her eyes are still in shock. Why is she so shocked? She's scaring Jordyn, so I hope the shock turns into something else soon. "Thank you so much," she finally replies. Snapping out of it, her eyes being moving normally again, no longer fixated on Jordyn.

"And what a lovely home," Jordyn says. "You've done a great job with the place. I love the color on the walls and what you did with the kitchen. It looks wonderful." Oh my god. She's the small talk queen. Why did she say she as so bad at it? Jordyn could win a fucking gold medal for small talk in the Olympics. The kitchen looks wonderful… That's golden.

Mom smiles and says, "Awe, you're too kind, Jordyn. So please, tell me about yourself." And Jordyn talks about everything I already know: Her siblings, transferring schools, single mother (but didn't tell Mom about her father passing), childhood, etc. Every small talk thing you can possibly small talk about, they small talked about it. And there I stand, listening to two of the three women in my life, talk about pointless shit for an hour: The weather, houses, jewelry, complementing each other, romantic comedies. It's quite boring yet very entertaining seeing them get along.

Finally realizing the main reason Jordyn came was for dinner, Mom begins working on it, making chicken fajitas. Jordyn offers to help but my mom quickly shuts her down, saying, "No guest of mine will be forced to make dinner," and "Why don't you ever offer to help, honey?" directing this comment to me. She always looks so comfortable making dinner, why should I interfere with the thing that makes her the happiest? Cooking dinner for her lovely son. Doesn't every mother love this task?

We spend our time sitting in the family room, watching paint dry. Occasionally, we say a couple words to one another but nothing to break her focus on the family pictures that hang on the walls. Every once in a while, I hear, "Awe" or she asks, "Is that really you?" or she says, "What a great picture." Things that make my mom blush in the other room, knowing that the pictures have done their job.

Dinner rolls around soon, and Mom orders the two of us to sit at the dining room table, awaiting us are plates filled with grilled chicken and green beans.

"This looks lovely," Jordyn adds while we're sitting down. I pull Jordyn's chair out from the table and wait for her to sit, then pushing it in, continuing to show her I'm a gentleman.

During dinner, Jordyn and Mom continue their conversation from before, except this time, they talk about future aspirations, things Jordyn would like to do with herself in the next couple years: college, boyfriend, graduate college, marry boyfriend, find a job and then kids. I find it interesting the way she orders this stuff, but I'm not too worried about it.

Afterward, Jordyn has to go home because Tiffany has a late soccer game she promised she would attend. "Tiffany got the athleticism while I got everything else," Jordyn tells Mom.

My mom laughs because she says the same exact thing about my brother and I. "My youngest got the athleticism while this boy got everything else," nodding toward me.

Jordyn thanks Mom for dinner, saying it was the best meal she's ever had. I find this hard to believe because although Mom is a great cook, being the best cook in the world takes a lot of talent which Mom does not possess. It's nice of Jordyn to say, though.

I tell Jordyn to wait for me, and she stands outside by the front door. I rush up to my room, grabbing *Night Road,* Jordyn's second favorite book. At first, I figured this would be a nice present to give at the end of summer when life goes back to normal and we all have bedtimes again and all the fun will be gone. It'll be a nice reminder that this summer was really special, and it was because of her. And at that moment, I'll ask her to be my girlfriend and she'll say yes and then we'll kiss and we'll spend our senior year together, going to Homecoming and prom with each other and we'll do all the cute couple stuff like go to art galleries and I'll help her with her poor golf swing, even though I don't even know how to swing a golf club myself.

But then I remembered my life isn't a book, nor a movie so I decide to give the book to her tonight, after meeting my mom for the first time. This is special enough. I run down the stairs, holding the book in my grasp, opening the door and seeing Jordyn standing there right outside. "Close your eyes," I yell.

She does what she's told, closing her eyes on command. "Reach your hands out," I say, much quieter than I said to close her eyes. She reaches them out and I place her second favorite book in her hands.

Her facial expression changes, a look of confusion turns to a look of joy, almost like she already knows what she's going to get. "Okay, open."

She opens her eyes and sees the book at her fingertips. "Are you serious?" she asks. "Oh my god. Melon, thank you so much!" She lunges at me, hugging me. I lift her off the ground, like they do in the movies. It's a lot harder in real life, probably because I don't lift as much as them.

"You're seriously the best, Melon. You didn't have to do this."

"But I wanted to," I say back to her. "You need to realize you deserve a lot more in this life than you think you do. You're the best girl I've ever known, and if this present makes you realize that, then I've done my duty." I didn't mean to get this deep with her. I don't even know why I began talking after she hugged me. The truth is, though, she does deserve a lot in this world and she really needs to start realizing that. She's surrounded herself with the wrong type of people in the past, and it's time that she knows that nice people do exist.

"Seriously. Thank you." Then she tells me she'll see me soon and she waltzes off to her car. Driving away, Jordyn holds the book out the window, yelling. No words, only yelling. And I really hope she doesn't drop it because that would be a waste of $18.75 if she does. Not including tax.

August 10, 2017

I hand her the piece of paper and she begins reading. The sound of the water makes it hard to hear, but I can make out the words.

> I've decided to write my summer English assignment on the most beautiful place I've been to with the most beautiful girl on the planet. Hopefully, this will qualify as a "fictional story" although it's not. But I will fabricate some parts of the story, so some parts may be fictional. You just must decipher which parts are and which aren't.
>
> I sit in the passenger seat of the car, speechless. I was told we were going to a safe place that is quiet, but all I see are run-down houses with their roofs torn apart and their wood chipped. No children are on the sidewalks, running around like children are supposed to. I see grown adults walking instead, brown paper bags in their hands with their faces hanging low, looking dark and gloomy with white and black people fighting near the local supermarket. I begin wondering why they are fighting and if the police will show up soon and stop it. Then, I realize that the brown paper bag filled with a mystery object may be the reason why they're fighting and it's the cause of their faces looking so dark and gloomy. It might be the reason why these people are so mad at the world.

We continue driving. I keep looking out the window where now I see houses that are painted a poor shade of their owner's least favorite color. Couples that are probably in their late twenties are walking the sidewalk, holding hands. These couples are not holding brown paper bags but holding ice cream cones, a look of happiness on their faces. I begin wondering if these couples are aware of the fighting that is happing ten minutes down the road. Their faces might change if they knew fighting was going on. Maybe they would move and the houses they live in will turn to houses that have their roofs torn apart and wood chipped.

Still driving, we pass through a really nice neighborhood where children are out running on the sidewalks and old couples are walking their dogs. The homes are very beautiful and painted very nice shades of their owner's favorite color. Everyone waves to us and smiles. Basketball hoops are at the end of cul-de-sacs, where kids gather and play a competitive game, yelling, "That's a foul!" and "You were out of bounds!"

We drive further and further. I look out the window and no longer see signs of civilization, but only trees that surround us on both sides. We're driving on a very small road, only big enough for one car to drive at once. She pulls over on the side of the road and I begin to question whether or not she has the right spot. Does she really know where she is going?

The feeling of not being in control haunts me at times, forcing myself to put my trust into her hands. Should I trust her? Should I not? Not knowing what I got myself into, she begins walking into the forest, not saying a word. Silence is the only friend I have right now. I'm trusting someone I've known for a short while. No animals are out. The sound of the wind and a faint noise in the distance are the only things talking.

Looking up, I see nothing but green. The leaves covering the light blue sky that once was shining down on us while we were driving. The wind dies down, but the noise in the distance grows louder. I still can't make it out, but as we continue to walk, it grows more and more strong. Peaceful.

Drip, splash, sloosh. It's water. Trees become less frequent and the sun is shining down on us again. "Are you ready?" she asks, looking back at me. The sunlight is shining down on her face, making her eyes sparkle and her skin appear shiny. I can't help but smile when I look at her. She has this way about her, forcing smiles from people who barely even know her. Her beauty deserves to be out in public more often, maybe on billboards or even possibly TV. That way millions of different people would be smiling when they stare into her eyes. Just like I am right now.

The beautiful place that she promised we would go to finally emerges. A waterfall that is no more than fifty feet off the ground. All different sizes of rocks sit on the edge of the water, big and small, wide and thin. I look through the falling water, seeing a colorful rainbow peek through it.

I think to myself: *How come the most beautiful things in life are hidden?* This waterfall, hidden behind both bad and good neighborhoods. Hidden behind a road no other car has driven on and a forest most people are afraid of. The most beautiful people are hidden from people. Most people look at others, only seeing what appears in front of them, fake smiles and fake beauty. They don't care enough to look deeper, beyond what they see. The true beauty that lies underneath all the hurt and pain.

Her eyes, looking at mine. In that moment, thinking another pair of eyes cannot nearly come close to the beauty I'm currently staring out. Reminiscing about the time she told me her father had passed, the tears trickling down her cheeks, which were so rosy. The time when she first told me about the bullies and the crying in the bathroom, isolated from everyone else. The principal, refusing to do anything because she wasn't being physically harmed.

Beauty comes in all different shapes and sizes. Some people may look at her eyes and see the pain and hurt behind them. They may get scared and run. But me? I embrace them. The people who have the most amount of pain and hurt within them, also have the greatest amount of love. They've been in so much pain and have hurt so much, they forget what love feels like, forgetting what it feels like to hold hands and eat ice cream. Forgetting about running on the side-walk while they see their dad walking their dog, waving cheerfully. These people keep their love to themselves for so long. So, when they finally open up, it feels like an honor to be loved by them. You understand what they've gone through and how hard it was for them to feel that.

Sitting next to her, staring into the water with our feet hanging off the cliff, I realize I'm not only in love with her, but I live for her. Everything she does I find funny. Whatever she wears I find beautiful. Every annoying thing she does, I don't find annoying. I can't ever get mad

155

at her. She's always right even when she says she's wrong. I can't feel anything but love towards her. I can't help but feel I am alive for her. God put me on this Earth to find her.

I begin feeling bad for the people I noticed earlier, the miserable people carrying the brown paper bags. and the young couple holding ice cream cones. The people walking their dogs and the children running. Even the children playing basketball in the cul-de-sac, arguing every little thing. They may have found their happiness; I don't feel bad about that. But they don't have her—the girl with the most beautiful eyes in the world. The girl that brings you to random waterfalls in the middle of the forest. The girl that loves watermelons more than she does apples and bananas. For that, I feel bad for these people. For that, I'm lucky.

She sets the piece of paper down next to her, resting her hand on it to keep it from floating away. She leans in and very gently kisses me on the cheek. Her lips, so soft and warm.

"It's amazing," she whispers in my ear, before retreating.

"So are you," I whisper back to her.

August 11, 2017

I want to start working out. It's proven that girls like boys who are toned and in shape. Jordyn, who is different from other girls, is still in fact a girl. She cannot help but look for a muscular man who likes working out. So I've decided I'm going to change.

When I ask Jordyn if she wants to accompany me to the gym tonight, she doesn't argue. Of course, I didn't tell her the main reason I'm going. I just tell her I want to change my figure, not liking that I can see my ribcage. And she says, "I like your scrawny body. It makes you, you."

Jordyn comes around and picks me up around six thirty, and we go to a gym right by my house called World Gym. It's a funny name because I think it's only found in Ohio. I've barely looked at the gym while driving by it every day of my life. To be honest, I make fun of people who attend the gym on a daily basis. The type of person who doesn't have much going on upstairs so must go to the gym to make a name for themselves. These people like drinking protein shakes and eating kale. At least that's what people on TV eat when they work out a lot.

Neither Jordyn nor I are members of World Gym which means we must pay for their "day pass" which is like stealing $10 straight from our pockets. Walking in the gym is like walking in the zoo, and I am both frightened and intimidated—muscular men and women are all around us. Many of them have gallon jugs of water or cups filled with stuff called "pre-workout." The woman at the front desk told me they have a sale on it right now.

Sweat runs off these people's bodies like they've just exited a pool. Their hair soaking wet, and their shirts can be wrung out. They sit on these benches and machines, letting their sweat marinate on the bench and don't wipe it off with a paper towel or towel. The sweat just sits there until the next juice head uses the machine or lays on the bench.

The gym is divided in into two sections. The weights are on one side, where the people with the protein shakes and gallon water jugs are. Everyone over there is forty years or above in age and loves working out. I notice someone flexing in the mirror and can't touch their shoulder due to the size of their bicep. Their bicep is that large.

The other side is called "The Cardio Way," which I find dumb, but Jordyn likes it so I pretend to say what a clever idea it is. Countless treadmills fill the entire side, facing a wall with flat screen TVs hanging down. Jordyn explains to me there are two machines near the back that aren't treadmills, but they're called row machines. It's like rowing in water, except you're not in water. Jordyn says it's very difficult because it, "engages your core and works your upper body, lower body, and gives you cardio." It kills many birds with one stone.

Jordyn has worked out before, so she attempts to explain all the lifts before we actually start lifting. There's bench press, which is the main lift people do for their chest. Then there's incline bench press and decline bench press. She tells me they work different parts of the chest. But for me, a chest is a chest. People also do flies to make their chest look big to try and impress girls.

There're also multiple bicep workouts. There are "curls for the girls," which you use the bar like what bench press people use. Or there are things called dumbbells, which are little tiny little bars with weights on the sides of them. There are different weights like, thirty-five- or forty-five- or even one-hundred-pound dumbbells. I bet there are some people who use one-hundred-pound dumbbells for bench press, but when I tried picking it up, it was like attempting to pick up Thor's hammer. You can do regular curls or Zottman curls or "curls to press." There are so many different types of curls.

Next comes tricep workouts. Jordyn first introduces me to dips, which are impossible. After telling me about them, I try one. I put my hands on the bars, which are drenching wet with sweat, and try pushing myself up. I succeed at first, then, inch my way down, forming "ninety-degree angles" and try pushing myself back up, but with no luck. Jordyn does three sets of ten reps, which is quite impressive. She then introduces me to the tricep rope and proceed to do tricep extensions with it. Also, we go back to the same bench where we bench pressed and did another lift called close grip bench that works triceps.

Lastly is core. We enter this backroom that has mirrors covering all four walls. Jordyn tells me there are multiple workouts to work the core and get "washboard abs." We begin doing sit ups and crunches and then move to more challenging things like reverse crunches and "v-ups," which are much more difficult than normal sit-ups. Although very difficult, Jordyn makes everything look easy.

Not being able to move very well due to soreness running through my veins, I limp out of the gym, thinking I'm never going to do this again. How do people do this all day, every day? I barely make it through one session without collapsing and struggling for my breath.

We enter the car and Jordyn says, "Great workout Melon. How are you feeling?"

"Bad," I reply. I'm out of breath. I throw my arms on the wheel, resting my hands at the top of it. It hurts when I lift my arms up that high. With pain literally everywhere, I say, "Does this feeling of being a useless piece of crap eventually go away?"

Jordyn laughs. "You'll get used to it if you keep working at it. This is nothing compared to how you're going to feel tomorrow morning." Oh great. I guess it gets worse. I ask Jordyn if she wants to celebrate my first workout session with ice cream, but she declines, telling me ice cream is not a great post-workout treat. I need a granola bar or apple or something like that. But I know I'm never going to work out again. My body likes being skinny and my ribs like poking out. I'm not genetically able to get strong, but I have a suspicion that's what every skinny kid says who doesn't like working out.

August 14, 2017

There we are, sitting in Drew's basement, watching *Criminal Minds* for the first time in a while. Tyler Joseph is watching our every move, along with Josh Dun. I'm still sore from the other day, though. "I tried convincing Jake to come over tonight," I say.

"And?" Lindsey asks.

"He told me him and Jaret Miller and Ian and this girl he likes are going to the mall to find some baseball gloves for fall practices."

"Holy shit, he's actually going to try and play?"

"I guess."

I really wish Jake would come around more. It was nice talking to him about Jordyn that one day in the car. But, every time I try and reach out, he has plans already. He told me to keep him informed on all the up-to-date Jordyn news, but doesn't want to hear what I have to say. It's just too bad.

We discuss how JJ and Reid should be together and how the people who write the show made a mistake. In my opinion, Reid is the most loveable person on the show, and the writers never give him a love interest. One season he had a minor girlfriend, but she quickly dies in season 8. Once again, a melon doesn't get what he deserves.

I don't stay long and neither does Lindsey. She has plans with Hannah while I have plans with Jordyn. Lindsey is hoping tonight will be the first night they actually "do it."

"I don't want it to be too soon, but I also have thought about it ever since I first saw her in the mall." Lindsey's brain is unique. She mostly cares about her friends and family, but the other part of her brain specifically focuses on sex. Sex with anyone. If she's not thinking about doing it with someone, she wants me to do it with Jordyn or Nick or Drew to do it with their love interest—who's no one at the moment because Drew is "searching for the one" while Nick is "not ready to be tied down."

Not having seen Jordyn the past few days, I'm eager to spend time with her. Sometimes, you miss the face of someone you haven't seen in a while. It's only been a couple days, but I miss Jordyn's face, just like I miss Jake's fat mug.

She really enjoyed my story about the waterfall for my English assignment, saying it was the best thing she's ever read. She's extreme sometimes, like telling me it's the best thing she's ever read and telling Mom about how great the chicken and green beans were. Jordyn has always done that with me.

Jordyn meets me in the driveway, waving at me as I pull in. "You ready?" I ask her as she opens the door.

"Of course!" she yells.

We decide not to listen to radio on the car ride over. The windows are down, and our hair is flowing. Jordyn's hair gets in her eyes and she turns to me and says, "What the heck is happening here?" Then neither of us say anything for a while, soaking in the fresh breeze and the last few days of summer. School is closing in and we'll never get a night like this again. Jordyn riding in the passenger seat on August 14, 2017 is the night where Jordyn and I go to the movie with the windows down, not saying anything. Nights like these make me dream for summer to never end. Perfect weather and perfect summer nights with the perfect girl. It just can't be beat.

Stopping at Chipotle first, we order the same thing we ordered a month ago, when Jordyn still had Elliot and my love for her wasn't as strong. Sneaking them into the movie theatre is easy, past the teenager who doesn't want to be here and the ticket lady who isn't observant at all. My pockets have burritos in them, and she doesn't even see them. Got to love the movie theatre.

Theatre 4 is freezing, making me give my jacket to Jordyn. I would've done it anyway, but I suppose now I have a reason. She throws it over her legs, grains of rice and strings of cheese fall on it occasionally, forcing an "I'm so sorry" out of her. I don't raise the armrest, letting Jordyn make that decision on her own. She does the same, keeping the armrest down, separating us. The tension isn't high, but enough of it's there to be noticeable.

Afterward, I decide to take Jordyn to my favorite place. I drive into Old Worthington, stopping at crosswalks to let the elderlies walk across the street at an extremely slow pace. I don't tell Jordyn where we're going, like the way she didn't tell me about the waterfall. "It's a surprise," I tell her.

When we arrive, we sit on the bench, our legs barely touching, making the tension even stronger. The ice cream shop across the street is packed, a line forming out the door and around the building. The sun is setting, making the sky an orange-yellow color, a very pretty color.

"What is this place?" Jordyn asks. There aren't too many old people walking tonight. Families are out, instead; children holding their mother and father's hands. Cars drive by, with kids waving at us with smiles on their faces.

"This is my bench," I answer. "My bench is your waterfall. My happy place, I guess. The way the waterfall makes you seem younger, and invincible, reminding you of your parents' love. Time goes by slowly like you want it to. That's how I feel about this place."

The line of hungry kids and adults waiting for their ice cream is quiet. I see their mouths moving, but no words are coming out. The cool summer night begins to overwhelm me, overtaking me with its beauty. I look up, seeing the sky, and look down to my right and see Jordyn. Beauty takes many different forms, and I'm staring at least two of them.

A tiny smile emerges from her lips, teeth barely showing. The way my jacket looks around her body looks nice, almost natural. "This place is amazing," she says. "How come you have never told me about it?"

I've never thought about taking her here. I've never thought about taking anyone here, not even Jake or Drew, Lindsey or Nick. Not even my mom and dad and brother.

"To be honest," I begin, "I'm not sure. This place is too special to me. I've always come here, away from the world for a while. It's in the middle of the city, but I come when I need to escape from everything and just take a breath. It's a place that's known to so many, but only discovered by a select few. I stare out and see people and notice how happy all these people are. And I wonder if I was ever that happy at a point in my life. Or the elderly people that walk the streets with satisfaction on their faces, knowing their love can never be broken. I wonder if I can ever be that happy when I'm the same age as them."

Jordyn nods. "I understand what you're saying. But why do you have to be alone? You never thought it would be a good idea to show this place to your friends or family?"

"I've always thought happiness needs to be found alone. And then once you've found it, you can begin sharing it with other people. Just like your waterfall, Jordyn. You drove and walked for hours into the forest with no one by your side. You needed that silence and isolation in order to see how happy you can be. Reminiscing on the trips your parents made and how happy they used to be, you needed to do that by yourself before telling me about it.

"Memories and certain feelings are only special enough to friends and outsiders once the person who has them feel confident enough to say them aloud. Once you've thought about it for so long, then you share it with the people you care enough to tell. Because they can sense how special it is because of the way you talk about it."

I see her thinking, her brain turning. "I see. I see," Jordyn says, continuing to nod. "So you've found your happiness? If this place makes you as happy as you say you are, why haven't you shared it with anyone else? When did you discover this epiphany, Melon?"

"Well, that's the thing," I say. "Like I said, I've always thought happiness needed to be found alone. I was stupid enough to believe it for all these years. Yes, I've been happy with Lindsey and Drew and Nick and Jake. They've made my life fun for a long time now. But spending the summer with you, you've made me feel the happiest I've ever been." The most cliché thing I've ever said. "So this place. Like I said before, I've always thought about it as my place. I'm the only one who can see things and *feel things* the way they need to be seen and felt. But maybe I was wrong in thinking happiness can't be found with someone else, ya know? That this place can be our place."

The wind continues to brush through our hair. The sun is mostly set now, the sky appearing almost fully black. There are no clouds in the sky, making the bright, shiny stars extremely visible. Jordyn's face is difficult to see, but the stars and street lights allow me just enough light to make it out.

"That's really sweet, Melon, but you've always been happy. I just showed you what it's like to live a little differently. Not necessarily better, but different. So just don't give up on your beliefs because some girl showed you a different way to view life. No idea or opinion is wrong."

I turn my body so I'm facing her now. Her face becomes more and more visible as my eyes adjust to the darkness. "I guess. But you gave me the extra push. You made me do all those things that I've never been able to do. You came in my life and forced me to do things I thought I was never capable of doing. Not necessarily difficult shit, but shit that was too difficult for me." I cuss, but I don't care. And before I can continue my thought, she cuts me off, resting her hand on my thigh. I'm not even close to being aroused because her soft touch isn't being done for that reason. It's for something else.

"Melon," she says. Now her body is facing me. She looks different from the parts I'm able to see. Happiness on her face has turned into confusion and I begin to worry. I know what's coming and I don't want to hear it. I want to run from her. "You are the most amazing person I've ever met. You have made me realize a lot of things about myself. After Elliot, I didn't think I was going to be able to laugh or smile again. I didn't know pain could be so strong. Everything seemed dark and terrible. And when I called you that morning, you didn't think twice about coming over and spending time with me. You just came and listened and talked when I was sad."

I'm flustered; frustrated, rather. Angry at not only her, but myself. "Cut the shit, Jordyn. What're you saying?" I can't believe I just said that.

Jordyn slides further back from me, letting go of my thigh, staring at me like I'm someone else. Like I'm not the same person who took care of her after Elliot and not the same guy who cried with her at the waterfall. "Melon. You're sweet, almost too sweet. You give me compliments that aren't even necessary and overwhelm me every so often. You smother me. You do these *nice* things for no reason that just don't need to be done."

"When have I ever overwhelmed you? I'm really sorry I care about you. I'm sorry I want to prove to you how beautiful you are and show you how special you are. You've dated a lot of fuckheads in your life, Jordyn. No one has come close to liking you as much as me. Someone who sees what makes you happy. Someone who has understands you so much. You and I are a lot alike and we have too much in common to just waste that." I don't notice how far I slid away from her until I finish speaking. We're on complete opposite sides of the bench now, making it a very uncomfortable distance to talk to her. A distance that is extremely necessary now, though.

"Even if I did have feelings for you in *that* way, I can't put myself out there. I'm not 100 percent in love with myself still. I need to keep pursuing my love in God and trust he will soon find me everything, all the tools I need to find real happiness. I have a lot of things I need to figure out about me. I have to make myself happy before I trust anyone, even you, with my happiness."

Speechless. She hasn't felt anything the entire time she's known me. That's what she's saying. The first conversation we had about her loving melons is all a lie. Us holding hands walking through the forest is now just a fairy tale I need to forget. Jordyn telling me I'm the best, countless times, lies.

"So you've been messing with me this entire time? Ever since that night at the bar?"

"Anything I've done to you hasn't been on purpose. I really love spending time with you. You're honestly one of my best friends and I care a lot about you, honestly. I guess I can *maybe* see you in that light in the future. But right now, I view you as a person I cherish, like a brother who always has my back."

Jordyn is continuing to fill my head with lies. *I guess I can maybe see you in that light in the future?* I call bullshit. Also, Jordyn has made up a new level of being friendzoned, something more heartbreaking and horrible—the "brotherzone." I've heard of stories of people's love interest telling them they're not good enough and they want to remain friends. But I've never heard of these stories ending up like this, being called a brother.

The way she says it too. It's like having a heart-to-heart conversation with your dog. You never want your dog to hurt or feel pain. So its owner talks in a voice that's almost childish, a high-pitched voice that's hard on the ears. You drag out every syllable because you want to make sure your dog is hearing everything correctly. That's the tone of voice Jordyn is using. It sucks because I'm finally realizing everything all at once. In the last month, every sign I took as love has been fiction in my head. I've made Jordyn this angel that can do no wrong. But, in reality, she's just like everybody else. All the signals I thought were signs of affection were just signs of sympathy. And trust me, no guy will ever accept signs of pity from a girl.

"I don't know what to say," I say to her. I keep sitting on the bench, my body is no longer facing her, but facing the ice cream shop across the street, whose line has died down significantly. I notice two little girls, sitting on a wall in front of the shop, staring at us with their legs hanging off. They seem innocent. Their faces have no expression, but yet they keep staring.

"Melon. I'm sorry. I really am. But you can't expect feelings to magically appear. Compliments and gifts can't buy me. Besides, if I did end up liking you and we tried dating, I can't see it lasting. Friendships that evolve into relationships never work." That's clearly a lie. She's simply trying to justify why she doesn't have feelings for me. And *buy* her? I'm not fucking purchasing a hooker for a night off the street, I'm enjoying doing simple and nice things for the girl I care about. Well, maybe cared about.

"I would like to disagree on the assumption you just made. Friendships evolve into the best relationships. You've shown me more about life than I've learned in seventeen years and eleven months of living. You've taught me how to live and enjoy life and not just watch Criminal Minds all day. We know each other's favorite everything. I know what makes you happy and what makes you sad. I know your family and everything about them. You opened up to me and I opened up to you because we trust each other. So, please don't give me any bullshit excuses on why you can't be with me."

Jordyn calmly gets up from the bench, "I'm going to be in the car. It's too far for me to walk home. If you can, please drive me home. Can I have the keys?" She really has the audacity to ask if I can drive her home and give her my keys? I close my eyes in anguish, knowing that nothing can be the same between us. I put myself in that situation, understanding the risks that it entailed. There's no one to blame but myself. But she's running away from the situation, scared of this conversation?

I throw her the keys and say, "Take the car home. I'll find a ride," and remain seated, the same expressionless look just like the little girls across the street. Maybe they've had their heart broken as well. Clouds have come across covering the stars that hang overhead. Even the Lord knows that I'm hurting and God's brightest star has crushed my heart, making him want to cover the rest of the stars from my line of sight.

The bench, which was once so peaceful, has now turned into my darkest memory. The place where I can sit and find my happiness, has now become the place where happiness will never be achieved. Thinking about the memories with Jordyn, specifically, the waterfall and the way she told me about her safe place seemed so special. The way she walked into *my* safe place and told me the harsh truth she was feeling this entire summer. Now I'm unsure when I'll find another Jordyn Marie Wright in my lifetime, especially if I ever want to find another. Because the love I felt for her—the love I still feel for her—will never go away. Plus, it's not fair to try and compare anyone else to her, because no girl would ever.

Summer's down to its last week or two, and the late-night drives and sleeping in is almost finished. I've been spending a lot of time with Mom lately, trying to get me ready for my senior year, buying me notebooks, pencils, binders, and everything school demands. Mom even bought me colored pencils and markers in case of a "color pencil and marker situation."

My dad and brother's baseball season has wrapped up, ending about a week ago. My brother played a total of four innings, only having one "at-bat" the entire summer. His morale remains high, though, explaining to me that "half the team is going to graduate, and they're all really good. I have a really great opportunity next year."

Dad keeps grilling burgers and hot dogs for us. He always says, "This is my best batch, ladies," every time he finishes grilling. Somehow, he is always right. They progressively are getting better and better, and every time I finish one I sit in my seat in amazement. My father is a lot of things, but a liar is not one of them.

Spending so much time with my family has made me keep my mind off Jordyn. Yes, I was filled with rage and a passion to hurt her like she hurt me. But rage has turned into acceptance. I don't blame for Jordyn for not feeling the same way I feel about her. It's like I've said in the past, it's extremely difficult to build a relationship. It's hard to find someone who sees you in *that* way. I just convinced my mind that she had. I fooled myself into believing that someone might feel the same way about me that I do them.

The whole situation is just fucking pathetic. Honestly, I find it hard to believe that I did this because Jordyn didn't say anything that made me feel this. I got caught up in her beauty and her personality. People say this type of hurt makes me stronger, but I find that hard to believe. How in the hell will this help me in the future? Movies and TV always say how pain helps to learn life lessons. The lone thing this situation has brought to life is me understanding and realizing I must be much wiser. I can't place myself in situations where I'm destined to get hurt. Relationships hurt people, and I respect every soul who has successfully found their true love and married them and had a family.

I haven't tried speaking to her since. All I know is Tiffany had a soccer tournament for her school team this past weekend—Jordyn had told me a week or two ago. Jordyn loves to support Tiffany, so she went and watched and cheered her on. I can't bring myself to text her anyway; no way she wants to hear from me. And to be honest, I don't know what I would say. Would I act like that conversation never happened? Like, try and be best friends again? Or is everything going to be weird and difficult now? The exact situation I've been trying to avoid all summer.

Nick, Drew, and Lindsey have reached out to me as well, but I'm embarrassed to even talk to them. They provided me all the options, and out of all the possible options and all the possible solutions, this outcome was the worst. I never imagined she would actually dislike me for having feelings for her. So I've been trying to avoid them as much as possible. Friends care, I realize that. But some things need to be dealt with alone.

Jake hasn't tried contacting me either. His wild, uncontrolled summer with Jaret Miller and Ian is almost finished. I hope he doesn't come running back to us because he feels he can just "have his way with us." He deserves what is coming to him, and I feel like it's going to be something bad. I have to realize friends come and go in this world. I need to just find the friends that come and stay. The ones like Nick, Drew, and Lindsey who have tried talking to me and tried understanding. People who actually care about your well-being and love you more than you love yourself at times.

I'm hoping to find time and spend time with the rest of the fantastic four before we go back for school. The people I began this summer with and experienced what it felt like to live. The feeling of immortality while streaking through the divot filled field while the cops were shining flashlights in our direction and smoking cigarettes with one another, willingly. I still also love watching *Criminal Minds* and eating pizza in basements, ranking girls on a scale from 1–10.

I really need to find time to see them. Mom scheduled haircuts and dentists and doctors' appointments for this upcoming week. My week is going to be filled, but I have to find time for them because they're friends I will never forget about. I suppose relationships or failed relationships will come and go. You never know what's going to happen with them. But I will always know how happy my friends make me, knowing I don't deserve them. Yet here they are, always coming back.

August 30, 2017

The rain is pouring down, symbolizing that summer is near over and school is right around the corner. Senior year is less than a week away, and I am terrified. The entire summer I had control of who I saw. I held the power to avoid Jaret Miller and Ian and the rest of the jocks. But high school is fair game. I can't control who I see and when I see them. The power of control is no longer in my hands.

Jordyn wants to see me tonight. She texted me and called me days ago, but I decided not to respond. Finally, today, I decided to answer her. I want to put the awkwardness away. She shouldn't feel awkward and nor should I. So I agree to go to the bowling alley with Jordyn tonight along with Drew, Nick, Lindsey, and Hannah. Lindsey and Hannah are doing really well too. They've seen each other a lot lately, and Hannah isn't allergic to Lindsey's bullshit yet, so that's a very promising sign for their future.

Lindsey also mentioned that they had sex for the first time recently. "It was like having an orgasm with Emma Watson," she said. I got really jealous when she said that because I've always wanted to have an orgasm with Emma Watson. But don't worry, Emma; I would buy you dinner first. Plus, make you breakfast the next morning.

After all the appointments this past week, I managed to find some relaxation time with Nick, Drew, and Lindsey. We didn't do anything special, just ranked girls from 1–10 and watched *Criminal Minds*. I had forgotten how good the episode was with the Reaper, so we watched that one twice. They decided it was finally time to rank Jordyn. She is allowed to be ranked because she is not an ex and I didn't have relations with her, although I wish we did. I do not partake in the ranking and allow everyone else to do my dirty work.

Nick, Drew, and Lindsey discussed her for a very long time, ruling and overruling. The conversation became louder and louder with each category. I heard muffled voices because I decided to cover my ears, but when I felt a tap on my shoulder I knew the final reckoning would soon commence.

"This was a tough one," Lindsey said. "A lot of back and forth, but I think we got many precise and accurate measurements. We will not tell you the final scores in each category, but we'll tell you the final score we concluded. Drum roll, please, Nicholas."

And Nick's name isn't really Nicholas, but Lindsey wanted to add some dramatic affect before she told me what they ranked Jordyn.

Overall, they ranked Jordyn an 8.75/10, which isn't too shabby at all. I tried arguing and attempted to push her 8.75 score to a solid 9, but to no luck. I know she's really a ten, but an 8.75 is one of the highest scores we've ever recorded.

I leave to pick up Jordyn around 6:30. She wants me to pick her up in my car because "Your car is where it all started." That's what she told me on the phone. On the way over, the green Saturn is making some noises it's never made before, sounding like it's breaking down with every brake and every acceleration. I no longer can turn the AC on while driving because the car will sadly break down if I do. My window cannot be rolled down, because if I roll it down, it will get stuck. Dad tried taking it to a car place where they fix cars and have a lot of car parts, but the man said, "We don't have the correct parts to fix this sack of shit," so I can't roll the window down.

I see Jordyn standing on her front porch, waiting for me to come and pick her up. She's just standing there, looking pretty as ever. Her watermelon dress is in full force; the same outfit she had worn on the first night I met her. She waves to me, pretending nothing has changed and acting like it's the first time I picked her up for the movies that night. The anticipation I had running through my body and the honor I felt to be picking up the girl I always wanted to pick up. The horrible thing is I feel all those same feelings, but everything has changed.

Jordyn walks and opens the passenger side door, the wind blowing her hair, making it seem she's moving in slow motion, all those feelings of guilt and embarrassment rushing in me. She shot me down after I poured my feelings out, and knowing there's no possible way our relationship can be rekindled, I'm going to try my best.

"Hey, Melon," she says, entering the car. "It's been a while, huh?" Her voice is the same.

"Indeed it has," I say. "Indeed it has." The interaction feels different. We're trying to play it off when in reality, it can't be played off. It's something that must be dealt with. The tension isn't, "Is she going to hold my hand?" or, "What would she think if I put my arm around her?" It's not that type of tension anymore, but rather, "What are we going to say next?" type of tension.

"I'm really sorry about what happened that night," Jordyn says. "I shouldn't have told you like that, and I feel awful about the situation. The truth is I don't know what I'm feeling. I'm a hormonal teenager who doesn't know what she wants and doesn't realize what makes me happy. But I know I can't lose you. That's the one thing in my life that I do know."

Tears begin to well up in my eyes, but I resist the temptation. I cannot cry in this situation. I would look like a fucking pussy if I cried right now. "It's not your fault," I tell her. "You didn't do anything wrong. Sometimes the truth hurts, and I need to realize that things like this do happen in life."

Jordyn's face drops. "Yes, sometimes things don't work out like you planned. But not like this. People believe heartbreak is a way of life. Like, a rite of passage. But that's bullcrap. No one should feel the way I made you feel and I hate myself for what I did. I'm simply not ready to be in a relationship right now. I can't give myself to anyone."

"Can you please stop saying that? I respect the hell out of you, Jordyn, I really do. But you can't expect me to bring myself to believe in that bullshit. The truth is, I love you and you know that. You've known that for a while. And I'm very sorry if I overwhelmed you by the compliments and the present I gave you when I didn't have to. Loving someone isn't hard. It's the simplest thing in the world. You find someone you care about and you spoil them. You compliment them and give them gifts even when they don't deserve them. You hold their hand when they're scared and give them your jacket when they're cold. It's so many little things that you don't even think twice

173

about. But I'm honestly sorry if I scared you. I just don't see what is scary about that."

She doesn't say anything. Her head hanging low, looking at the seat beneath her. We arrive at the bowling alley, not another word coming out of our mouths, listening to the radio in silence. We're no longer two teenagers soaking up the last days of summer, but two teenagers deathly afraid of saying something that will make the other one hate 'em.

Bowling goes okay. Hannah beats everyone again, but not as much this time, only by eight pins, which makes Lindsey very upset. But Hannah kisses her and tells her, "It's okay. You got me next time." I find that very uplifting and very kind. She doesn't need to give Lindsey confidence. Fuck, Lindsey's the most confident girl in the world. But she does anyway, which is very nice.

I ask Lindsey if she can take Jordyn home and she says yes, only if Jordyn gives her a kiss on the mouth and Hannah punches her in the shoulder for saying something like that, and Lindsey yells, "I was just kidding, babe!"

"Thanks for the ride, Melon," Jordyn says.

"Of course," I answer back.

"Will I be seeing you before school starts? I need to know everything before I can spend a day at my new school. Who's who and what's what."

"I'll be here."

And Jordyn hops in the backseat, and Lindsey and Hannah and Jordyn drive away. I see Nick and Drew say goodbye as well. They ask me if I want to watch *Criminal Minds*, but I tell them I can't because I have a lot of thinking to do. I drive to Old Worthington and park far away from my bench. I need the exercise, and I want to pass by people as I walk to the bench. Smelling freshly mowed grass and dog shit, continuing to think where I went wrong with Jordyn.

Arriving at my bench, across from the ice cream shop, I sit down slowly. A couple of minutes go by without anyone crossing my path. Then, up comes a senior man. His name is Jim, a very kind man who reminds me a lot of the guy I've talked to before. I begin talking to him about the summer and about Jordyn.

"Then, I told her how I feel about her, and she didn't feel the same way. So I had my heart full and my heart broken in the same summer, and I really don't know what to do because she's going to my school now, and what if I see someone else talking to her and I get jealous?"

Jim seems concerned. "So what's your plan?"

"Didn't you listen to anything I just said?" I say. I don't say it rudely, but more in like a direct tone. "I don't know what I'm going to do."

"I heard what you said," Jim says. "All you're doing is feeling sorry for yourself and dreading on what you could've done differently. You need to wow her. All a woman wants is to be swept off her feet. They like being surprised. My wife and I were dating for seven years before we got married. I told her I wasn't looking for a serious relationship. I didn't believe in God and didn't believe in marriage. And a couple years later, I got down on one knee and married her. And the look on her face said it all. And we got married and it was wonderful." He's so happy telling this story. The smile on his face says a thousand words. Even though if he actually spoke 1000 words, he would most likely collapse from a stroke or something.

"So you're telling me I need to propose?" I ask him.

"Absolutely not. Just catch her by surprise. Show her what makes you stand out and why you're the only guy for her. Then she'll realize there's no other guy she would love to be with. That you're the only man for her."

I nod. "Thanks a lot, Jim. You've helped a lot."

We sit there and talk about him and his wife. How happy they are together. How he wakes her up every morning with breakfast by her bedside. How she cooks him dinner every night, making him two margaritas with it as well.

Jim is a good gentleman, the type of guy that's rare these days. He's the kind of man you wish you knew growing up, just to see what kind of shenanigans he got into. He's also the kind of guy you wish the best for. Life can't be easy for Jim, so when he goes home to his wife and they lay next to each other on their bed, I hope he can rest peacefully while not being sore and worrying about shit he doesn't need to worry about.

When Jim finally reaches his feet and takes his cane to walk away, I thank him for what he had to say. He was very kind, giving me a lot to think about. Nothing more important than, *How do I wow Jordyn?*

I'm left sitting there, noticing the cracks in the road and wondering why there are cracks in the road. Isn't there someone that's job is to repair cracks in the road? There are cracks on almost every road in Worthington, which is so frustrating. Someone needs to complain about it to the "higher-up" to get it fixed.

A car is driving very fast down the road but is very far away. It's dark now, but its headlights are not on. The car is weaving from left to right, only appearing in my line of view due to the overlyingstreet lights from time to time. I hear screaming and people yelling, "Slow down!" and, "Pay attention!"

It's closer now, getting closer every second with every weave of the road. I remain sitting and watching, eyes fixated on how the car is weaving. I take a quick look across way, seeing the line that's out the door of the ice cream shop is also looking. Parents are yelling and children are crying. The car is moving at an extremely fast rate, not abiding by the 25 mph zone.

The temperature is perfect, making me not quite chilly, but comfortable. And yet goosebumps cover all the way up and down my arms. A shiver, runs through my whole body, finishing at my shoulders.

I want to stop thinking about Jordyn. And eventually I will. Actually, I don't want to stop *thinking* about her, *per se*, but just thinking about her in a manner I shouldn't. I can no longer fantasize about her, I can only imagine what life will be like with her sitting next to me in study hall and ditching class to get McDonalds and her being in my prom group. Except she wouldn't be my date, she would only be in my group.

But all that bullshit leaves my head when I suddenly notice the car is no longer weaving, but moving in a perfect, straight line.

Right at me.

I freeze. My body is now shaking. I'm cold. I can't control my limbs. A deer in the headlights. The deer I saw walking to the waterfall. The waterfall. So beautiful and so warm. Where her parents fell in love. My parents. Such kind and loving sweet souls. Being dad's boy all those years ago. Mom. Always loving me. Love. Nick, Drew and Lindsey. Taking care of me when I needed it the most. Especially this summer. This summer. Where I met Jordyn. The one who taught me how to do things that aren't necessarily comfortable doing. But to never feel ashamed of who I am.

A *Watermelon.*

*****

September 2, 2017

When the clock begins yelling at me, my eyes struggle to adjust, causing my vision to be extremely blurry. I'm unsure if it's because I'm still half-asleep, or the fact I've been crying for a few days straight and my eyes need more rest. It's really hard to believe something like this happens to someone like him, a person who truly doesn't do anything but care for other people. God works in a lot of ways, and I understand he's testing me and everyone that's affected by this; I'm just not so sure how yet.

When Lindsey texted me what happened, a million different thoughts crossed my mind, but none more important than, "Is my friend okay?" I can ask God why he did this or ask him if I can do anything to help, but every question will lead to another question. God has chosen a path for all of us, no path being the same for two people. Only He knows what will happen to Melon. All I can ask myself right now is, "Is my friend going to be okay?"

The worst part about all of this is not being able to see him. All of the details about his injuries are still unclear and hazy, but Susan put on Facebook:

> Thank you for all the prayers and well wishes. Our boy is going through a lot and appreciates EVERYONE's support. He has some pretty serious injuries, but nothing he can't get through. We ask for no visitors at this time because we don't want to overwhelm him and force him into any pressure situations. Please continue to keep us in your prayers and we'll update you as soon as we know anything more.

That is the only piece of information I have. Everything we've been through over the past month and a half, all of the memories we've made, were they all pointless? We didn't take any pictures, capturing the moments of time we took these adventures and time spent together, zero documentation we were even friends this summer. The only thing we have are the memories with each other, and hopefully, that alone can help him push through and be okay.

I don't necessarily agree with, "We don't want to overwhelm him and force him into any pressure situations," because I think that seeing friends would be beneficial to his recovery. Maybe it's because it's still kinda fresh and only happened a few days ago, but it would be lit if we can see him, especially because I left things on not-so-good terms.

I'm very frustrated with myself with the way everything played out. The last thing I wanted to do was hurt him the way I did. Melon is probably the nicest and kindest person who I know, which makes everything so much harder. No, I don't feel guilty for not being *into* him, but yes, I feel guilty about how everything went down. How was I supposed to assume Melon would be into me, especially after Elliot and I broke up? I was heartbroken and extremely vulnerable, and he was there for me. He saw me at my worst and didn't question his feelings toward me...not many people are like that.

Not many people deserve the love he gave me. The last time I saw him, he said, "Loving someone isn't hard, it's the simplest thing in the world." I'm still trying to comprehend this because for me, loving someone is terrifying. How could I spoil someone if I don't feel worthy of getting spoiled? How do I put everything I have into someone when I don't feel like I'm *enough?*

Loving someone isn't very simple, it's exhausting. Didn't Melon ever get tired of my company? Didn't he ever complain to his parents about me? Has he ever gone to sleep thinking about someone else? I hope he did because I don't deserve all those things.

Even if I'm ready to love, I can't live up to Melon's expectations. He puts me on this pedestal, relying on me to bring him happiness. I can't be that person. That's way too much pressure to put on someone. Happiness can't be found through someone else. Happiness

179

can't be found *with* someone else. Happiness needs to be discovered alone, not to please anyone but yourself.

While dating Elliot, I felt used and hurt, like I wasn't even there at times. Throughout the time we were dating, he had this way to make me feel bad about everything. I would feel so guilty if I chose the wrong place to eat, wrong place to shop, every choice I made seemed wrong.

Yet I stayed with him because he convinced me I was happy. Sometimes, it seemed like I was truly happy. Not because of the flowers or dinner dates. Not because of the conversations or the occasional laugh. I convinced myself I needed to date to feel normal, to talk about it with my friends and discuss it at the dinner table with my family. All the popular TV shows and the movies in Hollywood all trick you into believing it's someone else's responsibility to help yourself find joy. Society and certain social stigmas try to influence people by manipulating them into perceiving dating as a top tier goal in life.

I'm not quite sure what happiness is, that's why I need time. But as horrible as it may seem, I know I can't date Melon. He's reliable and sincere—traits that aren't typical in a guy our age. It's hard to explain. Some people aren't meant to date and some people are. This gut feeling tells me Melon and I don't belong with another. We can still make each other laugh and bring happiness to one another, but his happiness can't be reliant on my opinion of him. That's not how it's designed to work.

*****

My bed is cozy, making it extremely hard to get my day started. If I spend too much time in solitary confinement, I'll go crazy thinking about what I could've done differently and blame everything on myself, which isn't the greatest idea. My mom said something about shopping for school supplies today which would be fun. I haven't spent a ton of time with my family this summer, so it'll be nice. I would ask for a girl day, but then Mom would be frustrated with me I didn't want to include Jeff, and when I try to argue Jeff doesn't even want to come in the first place, she would be disappointed in me for leaving him out.

Tiff has been very helpful as of late. When I get sad, she comes in and lays on my bed with me, which has been happening more frequently. Then she tries to persuade me to transfer back to my old school and finish out my high school career with her, but to no avail. I really can't stand that school with the fakest of the fake roaming the halls. My old friends are not nice people, so why should I continue going to a place where I'm constantly unhappy?

Family time is really comforting. With no dad in the picture, I thought the balance of the family scale would be wonky; Mom would be too invested in herself and walk around all sad and miserable instead of taking care of us. Luckily, Tiff and I convinced her to partake in some group therapy sessions with other people like her. The people who were unlucky enough to have their spouses die of cancer. Those therapy sessions and church really helped her.

Church is something I'm really looking forward to. Tomorrow's Sunday, which means things will start going back to normal, which means I'll start getting back to my daily routine. Rather than sitting here and crying the day away, my family will go to church with me, directly by my side, appreciating what God has done for us. People don't like how God works sometimes, constantly blaming him for all evil in the world. That's nowhere near the truth and God shouldn't be blamed for the Devil's work. Everyone who doesn't believe in God needs to realize this life is only temporary. We need to strive toward moving to heaven because that is the ultimate goal in life—continue passing God's message and ultimately live like him, selfless and considerate of others.

"Jord, you doing okay?!" my mom yells from the other side of the door. She typically lets me have my space down in the basement but realizes I haven't been the best me these past few days, so she's doing her mom duty.

"Yes," I say, trying my best to seem like I'm fully awake.

"Come on, honey. Let's get out of bed and begin our day. We have some fun stuff planned." Moms have this way about them to make it seem everything is so genuine. Her voice is soft, like she's worried about me, but not too worried. Enough for me to notice, but not enough for me to get frustrated and shut down.

When someone asks me, "Are you doing okay?" I get more and more frustrated. Clearly, I'm not, so when they continue asking if "I'm okay," it's extremely aggravating. I know they're trying to help, but it doesn't, and people need to start realizing that.

"I'm coming," I tell my mom, rolling out of bed.

After throwing some clothes on that don't match, I open my bedroom door and see my mom and Tiff waiting for me, a smile on their faces. It's nice to see them smile, especially because I can't muster up enough confidence to put one on myself.

"You ready to conquer the day?" Tiff asks, taking my hand and pulling me with her as she begins walking.

"I think so," I answer back.

*****

To my surprise, only Tiff and I go shopping with Mom. To quote Mom, she says, "I want to spend time with my oldest and favorite children, is that so wrong?" I'm fairly certain she's breaking one of the many unspoken codes of parenting, admitting to us we're her favorite two children.

Like I've said before, family time is essential. When we leave the house, our first stop is Coffee Expressions, even though we're getting it tomorrow to conclude the Sunday tradition. I don't know what it is about coffee that intrigues me because the taste of it is *eh*. It might be because I feel like an adult when I drink it. Coffee's the type of drink you read the paper with, not sit around the campfire telling ghost stories.

We then go to the nearby mall and get our nails done. Again, this is an activity that makes me feel grown up when I have a coffee in my hand. It's different than when I used to come here and get my nails done with my friends, talking about the high school drama that occurred earlier in the day.

I wouldn't even consider them my friends anymore, especially after what happened with Jamie. I'm not even mad about it anymore,

I just can't wrap my head around how insecure a girl must be to get drunk and sleep with your "best friend's" boyfriend. They say drunk thoughts are sober feelings, and Jamie Collins just solidifies that ole' fashioned saying.

I'm not a "girly girl," by any means, but getting my fingers and toes painted is nice. Tiff and I tend to do it every couple weeks, as soon as we spot our nails chipping from the last manicure/pedicure. Normally, I don't like people touching my feet. For starters, it tickles. Secondly, people who enjoy touching feet are disgusting and gross. Feet are the nastiest part on the human body, surpassing: butt crack, inner ear, armpit, and the good ole penis—it's filthy.

After my nails are painted a bright shade of red, we walk around and go in and out of stores, gathering the proper school supplies we needed for next week. A new school is always frightening, but a new school my last year of high school is daunting. It's good to know I have people there I already get along with and know, especially Melon. I'm really hoping I get a call soon, allowing me to come and visit. Not only to see him and check how he's feeling (physically, not emotionally), but to get the low-down of Thomas Worthington High School.

Tiff and I don't get much, especially because we're old enough to have all the correct stuff by now. We no longer need to get paper or notebooks because we have that stuff stashed away in all of our closets. We did get new backpacks and very pretty back-to-school outfits, one for each of us. I keep saying I don't need anyone to bring my happiness, but it'd be nice if Melon was next to me, telling me how pretty I am in this outfit on the first day of school; that's an ideal world.

When we're done shopping, we make our way back home, but not before stopping and getting ourselves Chipotle. I of course, treat myself with a vegetarian burrito, the same one that caused Melon to call me a Communist. Tiff gets chicken and Mom gets steak, very unlike her.

"I'm with my girls; there's no judgement here," she says. I would never judge someone on what they eat. You like what you like, what's the point in judging?

As we are pulling into the driveway, the vibration of my phone pulls me in and I see a text from Lindsey:

What're you doing tonight?

Excitement rushes through my body. They still want me around. The last time I saw them, bowling was a little awkward. I'm sure Melon had told them about our conversation and even leading up to that, told them how he felt. I don't want them to think any less of me. I text back as soon as I can, eagerly anticipating this text for a while now:

Hangin' with you? It's awesome to hear from you.

After snagging my chipotle and allowing my mom to bring in the rest of the bags, I receive another text from Lindsey:

Wanna come watch some *Criminal Minds* at Nicks? Hannah's going to be there ;)

Hannah's not the deciding factor, but of course, I say:

Absolutely, more girls in the group. I'll see you tonight!

Just when I forgot to ask what time, I get one more text:

Great, 6:00!!

6:00 cannot come soon enough.

*****

Nick really does have an odd obsession with Twenty-One Pilots. The rug by the front door is even the band, staring at me like I've stolen something. Unsure if I need to ring the doorbell or not, I knock on the door, which in my opinion is in between ringing the doorbell and walking straight in.

Drew comes and rescues me from the outdoors a few seconds later, greeting me with a hug. "God, it's really good to see you." Drew's never hugged me before, but it's nice because it reassures me there's no bad blood.

"You too, Drew," I respond. It really is.

Drew leads me through the door, past the family room and down into the basement, where I see Lindsey, Hannah, Drew, and a little chubby boy who I've never seen before sitting on a plastic-wrapped couch. I'm caught off-guard by the plastic, but I'm more caught off-guard by the temperature in this basement.

"Holy cow, how cold is it down here?" I ask them when I reach the bottom of the steps.

They look at each other and smirk, must be an inside joke. "How's it going girl?" Lindsey yells, jumping off the couch and hugging me. "How you been?"

"Better than I was yesterday," I say. "You?"

"Same," Drew and Lindsey say in unison. Nick is too busy playing a basketball game on the TV. I think he's playing Hannah because she doesn't say anything either. The chubby boy has his mouth open, looking like he's afraid to speak.

When I walk over to the couch, Lindsey rushes past me and throws herself on the couch, patting the cushion next to her, implying I should sit next to her. "Well, if you wanna be selfish, and make me sit here," I say.

"So how have you been?" Lindsey says. "Have you reached out to 'Melon' yet?" I really don't like it when she says this because she wasn't there when we made up the name. That's our thing, and she's trying to make it a joke.

Continuing to look at the TV and trying my best to learn a sport I've never really been interested in, I answer, "I didn't know we were allowed."

Lindsey and Drew laugh, even Nick pauses his game for a quick second and laughs. "Of course, you can reach out to him," Drew says. "If you're referring to Susan's Facebook post, please don't listen to that shit."

"Yeah, that's bullshit," the little chubby boy finally says.

Lindsey mouths, "That's Jake," to me, which totally makes sense because he's been M.I.A. since the beginning of summer, except for the first night I met Melon, when he walked over to the couch where I was sitting, at the bar neither of us wanted to go to.

"He hasn't reached out to me," I say.

"The phone works both ways, my friend," Lindsey says. "Besides, can you blame him for not reaching out?"

Ouch. Even though she didn't mean it in a spiteful way, it still hurts to hear that from someone you care about. I already feel crappy enough for what I did without Melon's best friends teaming up on me, but it'll sting worse with his friends accusing me of lying all this time.

"Please don't say that," I answer. "You have no idea what Melon and I did this summer. You don't know how I cared about him so please don't speak on something you had no input on." I'm not a rude girl, but that sounded like the closest thing to rude.

Lindsey responds, "I suppose you're right. I'm sorry." Lindsey apologizing?

The basement freezes. The game on the TV is still moving, but Nick and Hannah aren't controlling it. Jake's taking a moment to pause from his eating, and Drew's eyes are open wide.

"Did... Did you just apologize?" Nick asks.

Hannah laughs. "Oh, she's apologized before," she says, winking at Lindsey.

When the laughter dies down, I decide it's time to apologize for everything, including Melon and I's conversation. "Can I say something really quick while this game is paused. I didn't even know you guys liked sports? Melon hates them."

"Oh, we hate sports!" Nick yells. "Nothing makes me want to vomit more than sports. But Jake loves them, so he got this gem as a gift for me for my sixteenth birthday. It's a couple years outdated, but I can't lie, it's fun as fuck."

I've never heard Nick say this much before, so I let him finish before starting to speak. "I'm really sorry if I let you down because of my feelings toward Melon," I start, "Like I said before, it's between me and him, and I'm sorry if you guys took any of the shrapnel."

All of them looking at me makes me want to cry. I think Lindsey notices because she wraps her arm around me before I start speaking again. "I don't think any of you guys consider my feelings in this situation. You see your best friend hurting and expect me to change." A tear comes rolling down my face, when all of these memories begin to resurface as I'm talking. "I can't give you a good explanation on why I couldn't love him the way he wanted. Plus, I'm not trying to make this a poor Jordyn situation and have you guys abandon Melon. I just want to make you guys are aware of how much I love Melon, just not the way he fantasized I would."

When the tears really start to flow, everyone in the room sits up and scoots a little closer, reinforcing they're all here for me. "We see your feelings," Lindsey begins, "and I'm sorry we didn't reach out sooner. We didn't know how much pain you were in until this moment."

"It's been so hard, looking myself in the mirror, realizing I did the one thing I *never* wanted to do. Truly, I never knew how much I meant to Melon until he told me that one night." Semi-truth. Melon did so many thoughtful things for me, how could I not pick up on his feelings toward me? The only thing unclear—how strong his feelings were.

Nick chimes in, "It's okay, Jordyn. We always knew he was capable of appreciating someone; just didn't know the first girl he would be interested in would be the only girl he saw himself with."

Drew agrees. "Yeah, Jordyn, don't blame yourself for the way you feel. You can't control how someone feels toward you. All you can do is trust yourself and express your real feelings. Lying would've only made it worse and prolong the inevitable."

My crying slows down as everyone else says these kind words of wisdom. They have no idea how much this helps. "Thank you, guys," I say. "Has he been doing okay?"

"Hannah and I went down to see him today around noon-ish," Lindsey says. I wasn't aware we could actually go *see* him too. I just assumed "reach out" is only texting and calling. "He seemed okay.

He's pretty beat-up, serious concussion and a few broken ribs. Not to mention his broken leg and sprained wrist. He honestly looks pretty funny all cooped up in his hospital bed."

Picturing Melon with his fragile body all casted up is scary. A Melon I would've never thought I'd see in my lifetime, but still the same Melon who jumped off a waterfall with me. "He able to remember everything?" I ask.

"Yeah, I'm pretty sure," Lindsey answers. "He didn't say much because talking hurts his head. Any movement hurts him to be honest. He listened to me and Hannah talk about things he probably didn't want to listen to."

Melon has always been a great listener. When I called him in the middle of the night, he didn't hesitate to come over and listen to me. Listen to me talk about stuff he had no business hearing. All he wanted to do was be there for me, listening to me complain about my own problems. He's not a great listener; he's the best.

"Want to come with me and see him tomorrow?" I ask Lindsey. I would've included Drew or Nick, but I'd rather have another girl there to help me out if I need it. Plus, Lindsey and I have more in common than me and anyone else in this basement.

"I would love to be your plus one," she responds. "Can this lovely lady join us? We're in love so we're obligated to spend at least four hours of sunlight together." *Love* is a big word for a few weeks of dating, but I don't argue. I'm thankful I get to see my best friend tomorrow, accompanied by Lindsey, who is in her best friend trials.

When I've officially stopped crying (which is getting annoying because that's been as normal as going to the bathroom these past few days), Hannah and Nick go back to their game, Drew turns his head toward the TV, Jake returns to his bowl of chips, and Lindsey stays stationary, keeping her arm wrapped around my shoulder, consoling me, even though I hurt her best friend. It's nice being part of a friend group that cares about stuff you should care about. My friends not only care about each other, they now care about me, forcing me to put on a smile.

The basketball game finishes and Nick flips on *Criminal Minds*, a show I've never watched before. I don't want to admit this because

I don't want to cause any waves amongst the crowd. It's a really good show with a really good cast. I'm going to spend my time when I get home looking up facts about the show and its actors, especially this blonde one they're calling JJ. She's a very pretty woman.

One episode quickly turns into four. There are conversations here and there, but most of our attention is on *Criminal Minds*. Lindsey orders a pizza halfway through the second episode which arrives during the third and is finished during the fourth.

When I was teaching Melon how to live, he was showing me something even better. He was showing me how to do nothing, but still enjoy it because of the people I'm surrounded by.

The lifestyle of a melon.

September 3, 2017

As I'm sitting in church, Tiff's hand in mine, wearing the watermelon dress he loves, one scripture our minister says keeps replaying in my head. "Fear not, for I am with you; be not dismayed, for I am your God; I will strengthen you, I will help you, I will uphold you with my righteous right hand."

This not only applies to Melon, but his family and friends as well. God provides us enough strength to continue pushing through all of the challenges we face. He looks over us, protects us, and loves us, no matter the mistakes we make, and that's really nice to hear right now.

Church is very peaceful. Everyone assumes it's boring and dull when in reality, it's uplifting and pleasant. It gives us a chance, as a congregation, to thank God for all he does. I understand God isn't looking for our gratefulness and thank-yous, but I would appreciate a thank you if I bring happiness and joy to so many.

The music is also very calming. Today we listen to "All Creatures of our God and King," which talks about forgiving others and doing your part in the world, a song I don't know the name of, but was very good, and "Amazing Grace," which everyone knows.

When church is over, my family and I go to Coffee Expressions and fill our bodies with caffeine. The first day of school is tomorrow, and I'm getting more nervous. Hopefully, my visit to go see Melon will calm me down. But I'm less worried about school than I am about my friend, who's missing his first day of senior year tomorrow. His "last first day" before he moves off to college and meets new friends and forgets about me and the rest of our clan.

Lindsey texts me as my mom is pulling in the driveway once again, almost like she's watching my every move. It must be pure coincidence, but it sure is funny how she texts me as soon as I get home.

> Pick us up when you're on your way! Me and my lover will be waiting.

Gross, but I do what I'm told. I don't even bother walking inside to change my clothes, my mom throws me the keys and then motions for a hug. Unable to resist a mother's love, again, I do what I'm told and hug her. She squeezes me tight, saying, "Good luck, honey. Wish Melon well for all of us." Sometimes mothers' hugs are irritating and annoying, but when the hugs are necessary, there's nothing like them.

When she tries to leave, I resist, but then release her from my grasp after a few seconds later, knowing I can't live in the hug forever. I hop in the driver's seat, check my mirrors, and begin the trek to Lindsey's, but not before I buckle my seatbelt—safety first.

After reaching Lindsey's, she and Hannah are already outside playing hopscotch, a very underrated childhood game. That would be fun to do with my significant other when I get older, spending the day playing games we used to play when we were young and eager to get old. That day won't be for a while, though, not until I'm ready.

"You ready to see your boy?" Lindsey screams, walking in front of the car as I'm pulling into the driveway, messing up Hannah while she's trying to pick up the rock.

Trying to match her excitement, I yell, "Absolutely!" Truth. I can't wait to see Melon. "Hop in, and let's get going."

The ladies jump in the car, and before they have time to shut the doors, I start backing up and driving away, highly anticipating the visit in which I get to see Melon. He doesn't know we're coming, at least I don't think, which will make this visit so much better.

I'm tired of overthinking about feelings and what I could've done differently. All that matters is I'm going to see my friend today. He had something bad happen to him, and I need to care for him, just like the way he cared for me when I got hurt. Friendships can't be one-sided, and I'll show him our friendship definitely isn't.

The drive over is quiet. Lindsey and Hannah converse with another, sometimes asking me the occasional question to end an argument, "Which one's better, Kings Island or Cedar Point," and, "If you were given a penis for a day, would you want to have sex with someone to know what it feels like?" With every answer I give, one of them erupts, yelling, "I fucking told you!"

Children's Hospital is huge, making the parking situation extremely difficult to navigate. Good thing Lindsey and Hannah are here to talk me through it, giving me step-by-step instructions on where to go and how to successfully park my car (I can physically park my car, just didn't know how to get there).

A staircase from within the parking garage leads us into the hospital. A frightening-looking woman sits behind a desk, awaiting our arrival.

"How can I help you?" she says in a way that's not very welcoming. I understand she works at a hospital, surrounded by sadness and grief, but she has to be more upbeat to try and avoid the sadness and grief atmosphere. She's not doing a very good job.

Lindsey is the speaker of the three of us, telling the pessimistic woman who we're here to see. When she hands us our name tags, we all put nicknames on them. Lindsey puts "Bad Bitch," Hannah writes, "Newcomer," and I jot down, "Melon." A little more sentimental than Lindsey and Hannah, but it seems necessary, showing him how much I care about "people like him." More importantly, I want to prove how much I care about him.

When she gives us the floor he's on, we walk away, walk into an elevator, and wait. When the doors slide open, we walk out and walk toward his room. Again, good thing Lindsey and Hannah are with me, because I would be completely lost, like a puppy who's lost its home.

After arriving to the room, we sit outside the room for a few, short seconds before walking in. Glass windows allow me to look inside, noticing Melon's parents and brother surrounding him at his bedside. I've never met his brother before, but it appears there's a first time for everything.

Susan and his dad look tired. I hate when parents look tired, almost defeated. I can't imagine either of them have gotten much sleep the past few nights. If sleep for me was rare, sleep for them was impossible. Maybe the three of us can stay for the whole day, giving them the chance to sleep if they want; that would be the least we could do.

Then there's Melon, the boy who doesn't care going unnoticed. The boy who doesn't mind staying in on a weekend and eating pizza while watching *Criminal Minds*. The type of guy who doesn't care if he gets eight hours of sleep instead of going to the nearest party and staying out all night.

I reach down for the doorknob and swing the door open. All this time, Melon thought he was the outsider, not belonging in a niche because he wasn't able to "fit in." Melon was the person who showed me you can be yourself and appreciate what you have around you. Because of Melon, I have a great group of friends for my final year of high school. Because of Melon, I'm able to see how much a guy can appreciate and love me. And even though I don't feel the same way, doesn't mean his feelings for me didn't go unnoticed. I've seen the standard, knowing what I deserve, but only when I'm ready.

He spots the three of us walk in. His eyes light up, staring directly into mine. And behind all of these injuries, altering his physical appearance, I can see happiness, bursting from the seams as we walk in. I no longer see his parents or his brother, all I see is Melon, sitting there looking at me.

"Hey, Jaxson," I say to him.

"What'd you call me?" he replies, a smile emerging from his face, a soft laugh quickly following.

ABOUT THE AUTHOR

Tanner Cowgill was born and raised and is still a resident of Worthington, Ohio. As the youngest of four, Tanner was the last to go through college and attended Wittenberg University where he was also a member of the basketball team. Reading and writing has always been his passion outside of athletics. Authors like John Green, Stephen Chbosky, and Krystal Sutherland are a huge motivator for Tanner and were influential to his novel, *Watermelon Guy*. When Tanner's not reading or writing, he is happily enjoying his job, educating the youth of America while teaching his fourth-grade class in Columbus, Ohio.

CPSIA information can be obtained
at www.ICGtesting.com
Printed in the USA
BVHW071938130122
626175BV00005B/83